QUEENS OF CYBERSPACE

AMNESTY

Clancy Teitelbaum

EPIC
Press

Amnesty
Queens of Cyberspace: Book #4

Written by Clancy Teitelbaum

Copyright © 2016 by Abdo Consulting Group, Inc.

Published by EPIC Press™
PO Box 398166
Minneapolis, MN 55439

Printed in the United States of America.

Cover design by Laura Mitchell
Images for cover art obtained from iStockPhoto.com
Edited by Jennifer Skogen

LIBRARY OF CONGRESS CATALOGING-IN-PUBLICATION DATA

Teitelbaum, Clancy.
Amnesty / Clancy Teitelbaum.
p. cm. — (Queens of cyberspace; #4)
Summary: The Pyxian-Altairi war is over, yet the victory the girls have won is spoiled
by Ramses's treachery. Suzanne, Brit, and Mikayla are trying to find a way home
when they receive a summons from the deposed king. Suspecting foul play, the girls
decide to attend to find out what other hurdles stand between them and making it
home.
ISBN 978-1-68076-200-6 (hardcover)
1. Friendship—Fiction. 2. Computer games—Fiction. 3. Internet—Fiction. 4.
Virtual reality—Fiction. 5. Cyberspace—Fiction. 6. Video games—Fiction. 7.
Young adult fiction. I. Title.
[Fic]—dc23
2015949426

EPIC
Press

For Milo P.

Prologue

Three girls lie in an apartment, dreaming. They have dreamed a day already. Although for them, the day has felt more like months. Time is funny like that.

Take Suzanne Thurston, for example, dreaming on her bed. She's curled up in a pair of sweatpants and one of her dad's old shirts—something he got from a hackathon a decade back. The last time she spoke to her father was yesterday, by the real world's clock. Then, he traveled to New Jersey for a job interview. He checked into his hotel, texted her when he went to sleep, and again in the morning. Then he did his interview. It went great.

As soon as he steps out of the building, he checks his phone. It's been, for him, twenty-three hours since he last spoke to his daughter. He's feeling antsy. They said they would be in touch, but then Mike winked while they were shaking hands and stage-whispered, "I'll be in touch really soon." So Suzanne's dad feels confident as he walks back toward his hotel and dials Suzanne's number.

For her, it's been two months since she last spoke to her dad—since she was last in his reality. Her ringtone is "Nayru's Song" from *Zelda: Oracle of Ages*.

She's meant to change the ringtone. She hasn't played a Zelda game in five years. She couldn't guess where her old Game Boy is stashed. Her room is cluttered, to put it politely, but no more so than the rest of the house. In fact, whatever tidiness exists in the apartment is directly attributable to Suzanne. Her father doesn't handle chores well.

In the same spirit of politeness, Suzanne's father is distracted. But who isn't distracted? Suzanne herself has to juggle chores and school with life's more pleasant distractions. Her best friends, Brit Acosta and Mikayla Watkins, are also in her cluttered room. Neither of them hear "Nayru's Song" either. They're all dreaming the same dream Suzanne dreams, all hooked up to the TII—the Total Immersion Interface.

The TII is a helmet over their heads, projecting virtual reality to their entranced brains. Suzanne's dad and mom designed the TII, but it was Suzanne who repurposed it as a gaming console. And it was Suzanne who built Io, the virtual world holding her and her friends' minds, the dream they can't stop dreaming.

Twenty-three hours they've spent dreaming in the real world, long enough for their empty stomachs to start to complain. "Nayru's Song" begins to play again, its chiptune melody harmonizing with rumbling stomachs and half-muttered dream utterances.

Suzanne's dad leaves a voicemail. Before he left town, he got into a fight with his daughter, or as close as they ever get to fighting. That worries him.

It's not like her to not pick up. But he rationalizes that she's mad. She's a sixteen-year-old girl. Give it another day and she'll calm down soon enough.

His math's a little off. For Suzanne, running on Io time, the calming-down day came and went a couple of months ago. He doesn't know she's in Io or that she's been using the TII for the last year to work on a game. All he wants is to talk to his daughter and share some of his excitement. He finishes the message with, "I love you," wondering if kids still check their voicemail.

Suzanne's phone beeps, voicemail received. She doesn't hear. She hasn't heard any of the calls she's gotten while she's been in Io. Mikayla and

Brit have likewise missed calls. None of them see the number of missed calls and unanswered texts piling up as their sojourn from reality stretches into hour twenty-four.

What they see and hear, at that moment, and what they've been seeing and hearing for the preceding day is Io. The TII is called the Total Immersion Interface for a reason: it's totally immersive. The helmet blocks off all sights and sounds of reality. In its place, the TII produces a reality of its own, beamed directly into the user's head.

Suzanne designed that reality to be the best game she could make. It's still in beta testing and a few kinks need to be worked out. The loot drops aren't fully randomized. The experience system has gone a little wonky and some of the AI is weird.

Also, none of the girls can log out.

The TII runs off dream power, to put it simply. And like a dream, anyone who knows they're in the TII has some amount of control over what they dream. Suzanne's big innovation was figuring out how to feed the same dream to everyone, instead of each girl using her own.

She should have tested the program more. She knows that. She was using technology she didn't fully understand to do something completely unprecedented. Of course she should have been more careful.

But who can blame her? Every test went off without a major glitch. In her shoes, standing on the precipice of another world, who wouldn't take the next step forward? Who wouldn't jump into a dream and bring their two best friends with them?

Now they can't wake up. Suzanne deserves a lot of credit. She left herself a backdoor out of the game—two access points where she can hack the game from within. But in classic game fashion, just because she knows where to go doesn't mean she can get there. The three of them have been running from one end of Io to the other, looking for a way into the hack points and back to reality. They've quested for royalty, hunted monsters, and fought in wars. They're heroes of the realm and wanted criminals. They've done and seen things Suzanne never imagined, battling for their lives.

And yet they never left Suzanne's room. Suzanne lies on her bed. Brit is sprawled on a beanbag. Mikayla is slumped in a desk chair, her weight having spun it halfway around. Of the three girls, only she entered Io sitting up.

A phone rings—Mikayla's this time. She was supposed to be at a basketball game last night and her parents are becoming frantic. They're worried about their little girl. If only they knew.

In reality, her phone rings to voicemail and Mikayla never hears.

In Io, in the dream, she wakes up.

Chapter 1

Mikayla missed exhaustion. It was how she went to sleep at night. Had she given the previous day her all? If she was tired as she fell into bed, then yes, she knew she had. Each morning she woke up a minute before her alarm. She was dressed and at the breakfast table with time to kill.

Of course, her mother was always up earlier. She worked the early shift at the hospital and was normally on her way out the door when Mikayla made it downstairs. Quick *I love you*'s, quick updates on the dinner situation, and then Mikayla waved goodbye.

Her mom was already in her scrubs. No need to waste time changing.

Then she repeated the act with her dad, only this time Mikayla was at the door. He'd enter the breakfast room as Mikayla shouldered on her backpack.

"Practice today?"

She'd nod, swallowing the last morsel of toast.

"When are you growing your hair back out?"

She'd shrug. He'd unfold the newspaper and say goodbye while he skimmed the sports section.

Then school—whatever that was—then cheerleading practice. She fell back into the arms of Daisy and Hannah, holding her body straight as a board as they lifted her into the air. Behind her the rest of the squad formed a pyramid. Daisy and Hannah boosted her on top.

The pyramid crumbled, collapsing underneath her. Mikayla fell. She landed on her hands and knees, her bones jarring against the hardwood floor.

"Again," Coach Foster commanded, a tyrant with her whistle. The squad tried again. When they got it right, Coach Foster ordered them to hold their position. Mikayla perched on top of the pyramid, stabilized by drilling and teamwork, and exhaled. She threw her arms out at her sides and presented her accomplishment to an imaginary audience—at games, to a real audience, who would then really cheer and sing along to Perry Hall High's fight song.

Sometimes, during practice, Coach would say they could stop, that they'd done well. And Mikayla would know that was true by the sweat on her skin, the drumming of her pulse. Then she would be exhausted. She would go home, shower and eat dinner, exchange a quiet version of her day with her parents. Then she would be asleep.

Or she'd go to Suzanne's, pretending it was some bonding thing for the team, and burn the night gaming, passing out when her brain was fried.

Either way, Mikayla was used to going to sleep exhausted. She still wasn't used to the sensation of Io. Here she was never exhausted, never even weary. If she skipped too many days of sleep her brain would kind of glaze over, but a catnap was enough to end that feeling. In Io she never felt that deep, satisfying yearning for a pillow. That basic structure was gone from her days.

She was asleep until she wasn't. She also missed drowsiness. In reality she had a private minute before her alarm went off. In Io she was fully awake so quickly it disoriented her.

Mikayla never felt fully rested, waking up like that. She sighed, sitting up in the rigid Altairi bed. Here she was in Ramses's old digs, the fanciest castle in the game, and the mattress was still like a rock. The NPCs had no concept of how a bed should feel. They only cared about how realistic the bed looked.

She pawed through her Menu, swatting the translucent blue rectangles until she got to her inventory. As she selected to equip each item, her clothes materialized on her body, perfectly adjusted and tightened. As a finishing touch, she equipped her swords, razor-sharp estocs, into the sheaths on her waist and back.

There was no need for a weapon. Zenith Castle was essentially empty. Her footsteps echoed through the hallways. The first time she'd come to the castle she was overwhelmed by the enormity of the castle and waves of NPCs currying for Ramses's favor.

The emptiness of the halls magnified their enormity. Each was the length of a football field. The ceilings were lost in their own high shadows. Mikayla crossed three halls before she got to the stairs, and then it was three flights down and another short jog before she reached the throne room.

The silence unnerved her. Io's soundtrack

had never just been footsteps before. There were always monsters making noise or NPCs hustling for a conversation. Suzanne had programmed outdoors with atmospheric white noise, filling the day with rustling and birdsong and the nights with hoots and howls.

In the castle there were only still stones and empty halls. Ramses had fled with half his court. The rest of the NPCs left on their own.

For a minute, Mikayla entertained a fantasy. She imagined herself taking on the mantle of queendom for Pyxis, just as Libra had asked. Mikayla imagined the halls of Zenith Castle were the halls of her castle. It wouldn't be empty but filled with NPCs waiting for her wisdom. But the halls were empty. And she had turned the crown down. She hadn't even tried for it.

A muffled scraping broke the silence. The throne room's doors were huge, as tall as the wall and symmetrical. Each bore the Altairi insignia of an orb resting on four pillars. As Mikayla touched the orbs they glowed blood red and the doors swung inward.

The throne room had little light, but Mikayla could see well enough. She had started the game out as a Ranger before advancing her class to a Swiftblade. That meant she had a Ranger's heightened perception.

She could see Suzanne hunched over and she could hear Suzanne muttering to herself. Suzanne's cloak was wrapped around her like a blanket. Her long black hair hung loose over her face.

This was, Mikayla mused, how Suzanne looked most mornings in the real world. Like a mess.

"Hey!" Mikayla shouted, her voice echoing. Suzanne looked up from the lock she was trying to pick and waved. Then she bent her head back to work.

Mikayla sighed. How long was Suzanne going to keep this up? Wasn't ten days long enough to admit she didn't know what she was doing?

Mikayla set off across the chamber, steering clear of Ramses's empty throne.

On the fifth evening, Suzanne set up a desk, chair, and cot by the door to the Oracle Chamber. Mikayla hadn't seen her leave the throne room since. The Oracle Chamber was really a hack point and their only ticket home. A green letter *H* glowed on the door, which, according to Suzanne, meant the hack point was still functional. The whole reason they came back to Zenith City was hiding behind that door.

It sounded simple enough. Suzanne was an Infiltrator, a character in the Rogue family of classes. She was supposed to be able to pick any lock. But since when had things in the game worked the way they were supposed to?

"Any luck?" Mikayla asked.

Suzanne offered a glassy smile. "I think I'm on to something," she said. "Usually when I try to pick a lock I have to do a mini-game, right? That doesn't happen with this lock. So I just need to trigger the game."

That begged for follow-up. "And how are you going to do that?"

"Um." Suzanne began to fiddle with the lock again. "Still working on that part."

No shit. Mikayla bit back the words but she had to wonder how long Suzanne was going to keep it up. Mikayla couldn't decide what was more frustrating about watching Suzanne—that Suzanne wasn't getting anywhere, or that Mikayla had no idea how she could help.

"Is Brit downstairs?"

Suzanne nodded, not bothering to look up.

"Want to come help with the Citizens?"

"Um."

Mikayla took that as a *no* and left.

Zenith City had been a metropolis like Zenith

Castle had been crowded. Now the Capital approached a ghost town. The fountains no longer ran in the plazas. Inns were boarded up, their proprietors gone. Where before the merchants' stalls were lined with gilded items, now there were a few more practical wares for sale. Even the great coliseum was silent. After a war, the remaining citizenry were no longer interested in violence.

They also weren't interested in Mikayla, or rather, they were interested in avoiding her. She could feel them watching her from behind the curtains of their opulent homes. She wondered if they resented her for helping to depose Ramses. She couldn't say and they weren't talking to her.

By the time she reached the elevator, Mikayla was ready to leave Zenith City behind. Her stomach lurched as the platform dropped away at a dizzying speed. Inside the elevator chute, she closed her eyes and tried to let the first frustrations of the day go.

She did the same breathing exercise when

she got in the car on her way to school. Inhale, exhale. Turn the key in the ignition and get on her way. The elevator slowed to a stop and the door swung open into the suburbs.

Zenith City rested on four massive pillars. The suburbs lay in the shadow of the metropolis, locked in twilight, thanks to the city blocking the sun. Yet it was the suburbs that were filled with NPCs. Before Ramses fled, the suburbs had been a haven for refugees. They came to their king seeking protection from raiders. Which they got, even if the king was the one responsible for the raids in the first place. Now the NPCs came from their villages and towns to get away from monsters.

The suburban homes had slanted walls and crooked roofs. On one block, an inn had been built like a Tetris piece on top of and between a row of merchant shops. Walls and doors had been built on the alleys, converting them into more living space. Nobody planned the suburbs.

They had sprung up within the perimeter of Zenith City's shadow so the NPCs could benefit from a city's protection.

That was one of Suzanne's better ideas. No monsters could go into a city or a town. It guaranteed the Citizens a measure of safety and it gave the girls plenty of safe zones where they could rest. They had all reached high enough levels that monsters were annoying instead of threatening, but it was still nice to be able to take a break from hack and slash.

Until the protection stopped working. Mikayla passed a cluster of Citizens holding spears made from table legs. The Citizen class was made up of non-combat characters, like villagers and merchants. All the combat classes were naturally skilled with at least one kind of weapon. Citizens were proficient with none.

Ever since their wards stopped working, Brit had tried to train them. The NPCs definitely needed the help. When Ramses left, he took the

City Guard with him, leaving the defenses to a bunch of Citizens. The makeshift spears didn't fill Mikayla with confidence.

Mikayla followed the NPCs to where Brit was training, by the edge of Zenith City's shadow. Unlike the NPC with which she sparred, Brit was a Dragoon and built for combat. She dwarfed the largest Citizen and could have probably beaten the entire militia with her arms tied behind her back. In the real world, Brit was short and skinny, not this titan in plate mail. At least her face was the same—round and smiling, framed by her dirty blonde hair.

Mikayla watched Brit shouting orders at the Citizens with a smile on her face. Even in the crazy world of Io, she always felt better when Brit was around. It was funny that Brit, who spent so much time in the real world complaining about rules and teachers, was going out of her way to teach NPCs the rule of combat in Io.

There was a loud crack as a Citizen went

flying backwards. Brit pointed the broken shaft of her spear at the NPC. "If I was trying," she said, "you'd be dead. Get back up and come at me again."

The two halves of the practice spear dissolved into pixels, destroyed.

Without complaining, the NPC scurried off to fetch more practice spears.

"I guess you can fight with the ones you let live," Mikayla said.

Brit laughed. "They're screwed if they go up against anything as strong as us. But they should be able to handle some kobolds or a gargantula or two."

She stepped closer to Mikayla, dropping her voice so the assembled NPCs couldn't hear. "Did you talk to Suze about the perimeter? Does she know how to bring it back?"

"She's pretty busy with her door," Mikayla said flatly. "She's sleeping in the throne room now."

Brit gave a disgusted snort. "Great. And I'm sure she's made a ton of discoveries."

Mikayla didn't really want to discuss how frustrated she was with Suzanne. She knew Brit was also ticked off. But wasn't that why they were down here with the Citizens? To take their minds off the door?

"Any monsters today?" she asked Brit.

"Just a little cockatrice. I let the Citizens handle it, but this one dude, Dustin, he got messed up pretty bad. I think he'll be fine. He's sleeping it off at an inn. I don't think he's going to show up for training tomorrow. They're all brave until they get hurt, and then it's back to being a merchant or whatever else Citizens do."

Mikayla crossed her arms. "I think they hang out at inns and complain about how things were better under Ramses. At least, that's what they do upstairs."

"You should move down here," Brit said. "It would save you the walk."

A bell began to peal. Mikayla could pinpoint it as coming from the southern edge of the suburbs. Brit set the bell up so the NPCs could call for her when they needed help. She took off at a run, shouting, "Ready for some exercise?"

Mikayla didn't look forward to fights anymore, not like Brit. When they weren't trapped, when Io was still a game, Mikayla could go all out without worrying about the consequences. But now they had to be careful, even with monsters.

Still, Mikayla ran after Brit. Someone had to look out for Brit, and fighting monsters beat waiting around for Suzanne.

In the distance Mikayla could see a detachment of Citizen guards surrounding a komodo, jabbing at it with their spears. The lizard monster was twice the size of any NPC, covered completely in green scales. Its barbed tongue flicked out, gashing the chest of the nearest NPC. The leader of the Citizens—or at least the bravest—stabbed at the komodo's head with his spear, but the point broke on the monster's hard scales. The komodo charged forward and pinned the spearless NPC beneath its clawed foot.

Brit got there first. She didn't bother drawing her halberd. She just lowered her shoulder and bowled into the beast. Mikayla grabbed the downed NPC by the shoulders and dragged him back toward the other Citizens. "Take the wounded to an inn," she said, drawing her swords. "We've got this."

The komodo turned, and for a brief moment, Mikayla thought it was going to look for easier prey. But then it swung its massive tail at Brit. Brit grabbed hold and held tight, digging her feet into the ground. The two of them engaged in a game of tug-of-tail until Mikayla cut the tail clean in two. Brit stumbled backwards, holding her half, while the komodo wheeled around, screeching in pain.

With a faint pop, the monster's tail grew back.

Brit looked down at the half of tail in her hand, then back to the lizard. "I didn't know they could do that," Brit said. She laughed. Mikayla thought Brit was enjoying herself a bit too much.

Brit grabbed the tip of the tail and swung it like a flail, slapping the lizard in the face. With it distracted, Mikayla ran around the komodo and launched herself on its back. The monster tried to buck her, but she jabbed her swords into the joints of its two front legs. The NPCs' spears couldn't dent the komodo's armor, but her blades went right through. Mikayla gripped the hilts and held on, letting the komodo wear itself out.

It began to slow down, its tongue lolling out between its teeth. Brit grabbed her halberd from her inventory and advanced slowly on the lizard. It gave a feeble swipe in her direction, but she easily sidestepped its claws. One swing of the halberd and its head tumbled free of its body.

Mikayla watched her experience points go up.

Inside the pixelating body of the komodo she found the loot—scale armor and lizard meat. None were worth anything to her, but she could drop them off at an inn for the needier NPCs. She rarely found anything worthwhile in loot these days.

Now that the komodo was dead and gone, the Citizens crept back out of the shadow. They really were hopeless, Mikayla decided. Either her or Brit could have handled the komodo alone, but the monster was too much for five of them. *What would they have done without us?*

As if reading her mind, Brit said, "They're getting better. I know that sounds like bullshit, but they are. You should have seen them the first time a kobold came up."

"It's not just monsters," Mikayla said. "What if classed NPCs come by? They couldn't fight off raiders like this. Or, like, what if Ramses brings an army? Who's going to stop him from taking Zenith City back?"

Mikayla wasn't sure why the king had abandoned Zenith City in the first place. Now that he was gone, she wasn't just going to let him waltz back in. But with only the Citizens and the girls defending the metropolis, who was going to stop him if he tried?

"Oh! That reminds me!" Brit said, smacking herself on the forehead. "Ramses sent a messenger! I had some of the guards hold him at Hawthorne's. Want to see what he has to say?"

Mikayla stopped in her tracks. Ramses sent a messenger? Last time the king sent one of those it was a trap. Well, everything with Ramses turned out to be some kind of trap or trick.

"Did you tell Suzanne?" she asked. She knew the answer to her question.

Brit shrugged.

"She's probably going to want to hear this," Mikayla said.

"If you think you can get her away from that door," Brit replied.

"I probably can't," Mikayla said. "But you can always drag her down here if she won't come."

Chapter 2

"Come on," Suzanne whispered. She was begging. The door to the Oracle Chamber remained unmoved by her appeal. For the thousandth time, Suzanne navigated through her Menu to the abilities tab. She selected lockpicking from her list of skills and placed her hands on the door to the Oracle Chamber.

Nothing happened.

She sighed. *What time is it?* she wondered. Mikayla had already come by today—or was that yesterday? They were beginning to blur together for Suzanne. Her world was shrunk down to the throne room in Zenith Castle. Digital sunshine was quickly becoming as much of a memory as real sunshine.

Well, she'd always been an indoor kid. And she needed to work on the door. It wasn't like Brit or Mikayla were helping. It wasn't like they could help.

She exhaled in a heavy sigh and pulled her hair back. Maybe they should have stayed in Pyxis, after all. Leo had certainly been keen on the idea. But then Leo was an NPC and his imagination was limited.

They said goodbye in Vale. No, Suzanne said goodbye in Vale. Leo said other things.

The mountain stronghold was where they went after The Floating Eye. The Pyxians won The Duels, winning the war in the process, but Queen Libra had died. As Suzanne stepped out of the tunnel into the caldera that held Vale, she immediately noticed that every Pyxian was wearing black robes of mourning.

If only I won, Suzanne thought. Leo interrupted

her thoughts by giving her hand a reassuring squeeze. That made her squirm more. It had only been a few weeks before that when she had taught him about holding hands, and he had quickly become enamored with—almost addicted to— the sensation. The NPCs were quick studies as long as they liked the lesson.

Back in the throne room, Suzanne pushed back her chair. Was it time to sleep? She wasn't tired yet and nothing had touched her health bar. But if she slept then she could take a break from the door. It was the only way she could justify a break to herself.

She stood up, walked the five steps to her cot, and sat back down. She was moving in smaller circles. But that was just efficiency. That was just because she had to keep working on the door so they could all get home.

That's how she tried to explain things to Leo.

"We need to get home," she said.

"Of course," he replied. "And now that I'm

king, I'll find my wisest subjects to assist you, as soon as my new capital is complete."

Suzanne hadn't responded immediately. They were in Libra's old house in Vale. While Libra was the occupant the house had been unadorned, filled with only functional furniture. Leo had immediately set up a portrait of his sister. He had replaced the chairs and brought wildflowers from the pastures surrounding Vale in vases.

But he wasn't king yet. From what Suzanne could interpret of the Pyxian rules of succession, anyone could be the next ruler with enough support. Leo simply assumed, as Libra's younger sibling, and as the older twin, that the support was his. He was wearing the royal circlet that all members of the Pyxian royal family wore, usually just at ceremonies. Since Libra's death Leo had worn his constantly, his normally ruffled hair smoothed out beneath the crown.

Suzanne knew she couldn't dance around the issue any longer. "We have to go back to Altair," she told him. "We're going to leave tomorrow. I'm sorry, but we need to work on opening the Oracle Chamber."

Leo stroked his chin, thinking. He stared at her with those piercing gray eyes of his. He was sitting on Libra's old throne. It was a simple chair but it looked too big for him.

"Is there nothing to keep you in Pyxis?" he asked.

She knew he was talking about himself. He was thinking in binaries. Either Suzanne was in Pyxis or she was not in Pyxis. Either she was with him or she was not with him. If she wanted to be with him, she would be; therefore, if she was leaving, she was done.

"Listen," she said, but she didn't have a follow up. "We have to go," she repeated lamely, and then she left her house.

Sitting on the cot in Zenith City she regretted how she handled things. *He's only an NPC*, she reminded herself. No matter how much she had thought of him as something more. He was a non-player character. As soon as she opened the Oracle Chamber she would leave this world and leave him permanently. She couldn't afford to keep pretending.

But that didn't block her memories of his pained expression as she left Libra's house. She supposed it was Leo's house by now. Brit, Mikayla, and Suzanne had stayed that last night in Vale, just to hear the beginning of the succession debates.

The still-living champions of Pyxis assembled with other elders of the nation in one of Vale's inns. Besides Leo, there was his twin sister Lynx, the master smith, Rigel, the steward of Vale, Alphonse, the girls' old friend, Mallon, and plenty of NPCs Suzanne didn't recognize. Even though she felt like she had been in Pyxis forever, she had only stayed in Vale briefly. It made sense that its bureaucrats would be unfamiliar to her.

"We're gathered here," Rigel began, "because

we need ourselves a leader. Now we aren't deciding anything tonight, just hearing what anyone has to say. Tomorrow we'll put the word out about whoever we're leaning toward and talk with the people to get a sense of how they're leaning."

Suzanne could feel Leo, who sat next to her, shaking with impatience. How long had he waited for the crown? That thought made her even more uncomfortable.

But she wasn't the only one uncomfortable. Most of the NPCs looked unhappy with the prospect of finding a leader to replace Libra. The previous queen left awfully big shoes to fill. Suzanne noticed Mikayla also looking down, staring at her hands in her lap rather than the assembled NPCs. But what did Mikayla have to be so worried about?

She probably just wants to get back to Altair, Suzanne thought.

The NPCs suggested the obvious successors.

Alphonse's name was brought up, but the burly steward politely removed himself from the conversation. "It is not an honor I seek," he said calmly. "I am touched to be considered at all."

After a few more candidates were discussed, Lynx asked, "Does it have to be a Pyxian?"

Suzanne saw Mikayla perk up at that.

"Of course!" Leo said, a little too loudly for decorum. "We have watched Altairi run free in our land for the past year. How can you consider leaving Pyxis to the hands of an outsider?"

Mallon cleared her throat. The old NPC spoke with more composure than Leo, her years of experience softening her voice if not her convictions. "The way I see it, we're Pyxians. We ought to be ruled by Pyxians. It's as simple as that."

Lynx didn't press the issue further. Soon after, Rigel brought up Leo as a candidate. The prince profusely thanked everyone assembled for considering him. An hour later, when the meeting broke, Leo was the only serious candidate that they had. The rest of the NPCs present removed themselves from consideration, choosing instead to present a united front to the rest of the population.

That night, Suzanne and her friends had gone with the rest of Vale to see the unveiling of Libra's statue in the Oratorium. The huge domed building was unlike the rest of the structures in Vale. Instead of black volcanic rock, it was made of marble-like white stone, with a translucent blue dome for a roof.

Inside the Oratorium were countless statues. They filled every inch of the walkways that crisscrossed the building all the way up to the ceiling. Each statue was of a deceased Pyxian. NPCs, like other game objects, didn't leave behind a body when they died, so the Pyxians had to make their own memorials. Leo had pointed out his own parents to Suzanne on a previous trip. Now they were putting up a statue of his sister.

Suzanne had never seen NPCs in mourning before. She had seen humans in mourning only once.

It wasn't raining on the day of her mother's funeral. It was sunny, so hot that Suzanne could feel the fabric of her dress sticking to her body. While she cried quietly she couldn't tell if it was tears or salt stinging her eyes.

Mosquitoes buzzed through the eulogies, draining blood from the emotionally drained. Suzanne could remember slapping mosquitoes better than she could remember a single word anyone said. Half the adults were wearing sunglasses against the glare. She didn't know their names. They introduced themselves, expressed their sorrow for her grief, and their own grief, all in the same conversation. Suzanne was overwhelmed by the anonymity of the mourners and during the reception went to hide in her room.

The Pyxian funeral was nothing like that.

All the NPCs sang. A wordless melody, but a

42

melody all the same. The notes swelled around her, filling the cavernous Oratorium with a unified song. Libra's statue was carried in to the building on the shoulders of Lynx, Leo, Alphonse, and a Monk named Shasta, like pallbearers with a coffin. They set the statue down in the center of the Oratorium's first floor. Rigel sent some of his apprentices to forge the statue to the floor of the building so it could not be moved.

But the Pyxians were moving, swaying together in rhythm to their tune. No eulogies were offered. Each individual's memories of the queen spoke loud enough.

Suzanne was lost in her reminiscence when the doors of Ramses's throne room ground open for the second time that day. With a start, Suzanne realized she'd been lounging about instead of working on the door.

Brit entered. "Yo!" she shouted across the room.

Suzanne waved. Brit had only been in the throne room once since the girls returned to Zenith City. "Don't you have Citizens to train?" Suzanne asked.

"They just took out a komodo," Brit replied as she walked across the room.

"By themselves?" Suzanne couldn't believe that.

Brit grinned. "I might have helped a little. Anyway, you've got to come down. Dante's here."

Dante? Ramses's messenger? Suzanne wondered what he was doing here.

"We're meeting with him at Hawthorne's place," Brit added.

"I can't," Suzanne said. "I have to keep working on the door."

Brit hesitated. Suzanne could practically hear what Brit was thinking. She knew Brit thought that Suzanne was wasting her time, wasting all the girls' time. But Brit didn't say that. She said, "Come on, Suze. It'll still be here when you get back."

Suzanne responded by walking back over to the door, sitting down, and resuming her work.

"All right," Brit said. "I tried to be reasonable."

Sometimes Suzanne forgot just how big Brit's character was. She walked over and grabbed Suzanne by the shoulders. Suzanne tried to struggle, but she knew it wouldn't do her any good. Brit hoisted Suzanne over her shoulder like Suzanne was a doll.

"Put me down," Suzanne said.

Brit ignored her.

Chapter 3

At the elevator, Brit set Suzanne down. Suzanne stared at her feet, but Brit knew she wasn't going to make a run for the throne room. Suze might be stubborn but she wasn't that dramatic. Brit studied Suzanne's peaked face, wondering how long it had been since she had left the castle. The elevator dropped them down in the suburbs. Brit led the way to Hawthorne's house.

Hawthorne was the first NPC Brit met in Io. Though she liked Hawthorne, he reminded her of nothing as much as a goat. His beard was a tuft of white hair, long enough to curl over itself.

Hunched with age, Hawthorne got around by leaning on a stick, thus heralding him with a clopping sound. He had a way of squinting at you that made him look skeptical of who you were and what you were saying.

But if he was goat, he was a tough old goat. He was the elder of Oppold, a village which was the frequent victim of bandit attacks. The girls had fought off the bandits and Hawthorne had enlisted them to shepherd the people of Oppold all the way up the Grand Highway to Zenith City. It was a long road, especially for an NPC as old as Hawthorne, but he made it without losing anyone from his village.

When they arrived at the Capital, they parted ways. The girls went off to quest for and then war against Ramses. Brit was surprised Hawthorne was still around when they returned to Zenith City, but she supposed that Hawthorne wasn't going to split without his people. With the wards around towns failing, Zenith City was as safe as anywhere.

In their absence and the absence of the king, Hawthorne had risen to mayor, assuming a position not unlike his old one in Oppold. It was his idea to train the Citizens as a guard and he was also the one responsible for finding the first volunteers.

Brit visited the NPC regularly in the weeks since returning to Zenith City. Brit was never the kind of gamer to talk to each NPC in every town, but there wasn't a whole lot to do in Zenith City and the suburbs without the court of the king. Her visits with Hawthorne and his two grandchildren, Henny and Ib, broke the monotony of monster skirmishes. As much as Brit enjoyed combat, protecting the suburbs every day for a month left her aching for something different to do.

Brit stashed Ramses's emissary at Hawthorne's because she knew the old coot despised his former king almost as much as she did. Hawthorne lived with his two grandchildren deep in the suburb. The sun was perpetually blocked by Zenith City, visible only during sunrise and sunset. Street lamps lit the way, but in places where the NPCs had forgotten to refill them with fuel the suburbs were dark and gloomy. Hawthorne's position ensured that his home was always illuminated at least.

Hawthorne opened the door when Brit knocked. "He's in the kitchen," he grumbled, stepping aside to let them in. "And nice to see you, Suzanne."

"Nice to see you too," Suzanne replied.

Brit had to duck under the doorway to enter. She squeezed through the narrow hallway that led back to the kitchen. Inside she found another familiar, if unpleasant, sight. The last time she had seen Dante the Paladin, he had been delivering Ramses's terms of peace. Those terms turned out to be just a bunch of bullshit. When he showed up at Zenith City, Brit almost took him out on the spot. But she didn't want to give Ramses a pretense to attack the suburbs, and also, Dante was waving a white flag, completely unarmed.

Dante sat rigidly at Hawthorne's kitchen table, flanked by two of the more competent members of the Citizen Guard. A white cape hung from his shoulders, bearing the insignia of Altair. Several instances of the pillared emblem in the suburbs had been torn down or defaced by the Citizens.

The Paladin kept his black hair slicked back out of his face. As usual, his face was set in a frown. He eyed Brit and Suzanne warily, but did not so much as glance at his supposed guards.

He probably thinks they're a joke, Brit thought, squeezing in between Hawthorne and a guard. Loathe as she was to admit it, she agreed with him on that one.

"Dante." Mikayla's tone was icy. She sat across from the Paladin, giving him her cheer captain stare-down. "What brings you to Zenith City? I thought you'd be hiding with your king."

"My king does not hide," Dante answered in his flat voice. "He chose to reclaim his ancestral seat in the Fenlands. He regrets that his former capital has fallen on such hard times."

So that's where he went. When Brit and Mikayla had discussed Ramses's whereabouts, neither of them had ever suggested the Fenlands. Brit's last trip to the southern swamp had seen her stuck in mud and snared by vines; picturing Ramses in the same situation gave her no small amount of pleasure.

"A swamp makes the perfect home for someone so slimy," Brit said. "Why don't you slither back to Ramses? Unless you have something to say."

Dante put both of his hands flat on the table. "I came freely as an emissary of King Ramses, bearing a banner of peace," he said slowly. "I did not come to hear your petty insults."

"Then maybe you should just leave," Brit snapped.

Hawthorne rapped his stick on the table. "He did come here with a message from Ramses and we ought to hear his piece."

Dante gave Hawthorne a nod of gratitude. "My thanks, sir. I am glad to have a voice of reason in this room."

"Don't misunderstand me," Hawthorne said. "I've as much love for Ramses as I do for a gargantula. Say your part and then take your leave."

"Very well. My king has discovered a vein of Energite in the Fenlands. As the rightful ruler of Altair," Dante paused, waiting for some kind of interruption. *Who gives a shit who the rightful ruler is?* Brit thought, but she didn't so much as grumble.

Dante cleared his throat and continued. "As the rightful ruler of Altair, Ramses has decided to share his wealth with the rest of his people. He invites all the nobility of the land to a summit held in Fenhold, his seat of power, where they will discuss how to fairly distribute the Energite."

What nobility? Brit wondered. She had been all over Altair, from the Fenlands to the mountains in the north, and Ramses was the only noble she had met. If Ramses was a model of Altairi nobility she wasn't trying to meet many more.

"The king has allowed Zenith City to send a representative as well," Dante continued. "The summit will convene in one week's time." Having said the words he came to deliver, Dante pushed back his chair and stood to leave.

"So we're just supposed to hand ourselves over to Ramses?" Mikayla could hardly sound more skeptical.

"You are not supposed to do anything," Dante replied. "Zenith City is invited to send a representative to Fenhold."

"Whatever. What's stopping Ramses from taking whoever we send prisoner?"

"Ramses is an honorable king!" Color rose in the Paladin's face.

Mikayla laughed. "He's a liar. How honorable was your king when he cheated in The Duels? Why hasn't he answered for murdering Libra yet?"

"Her death was accidental! Perhaps she should not have risked her own life in combat."

"Really? An accident? So it was an accident that Ramses sent a monster into The Duels? That he made sure it would poison Libra if it didn't kill her in the arena?"

Mikayla was on the edge of shouting. Brit was taken aback by the anger in her voice. They had hardly discussed the former queen of Pyxis and she would have never guessed that Mikayla was still this upset over it. Brit knew Mikayla was the last one to see the queen alive, but she didn't think they were really that close. *Besides*, Brit thought, *she was just an NPC*. But she knew Mikayla didn't think that way.

To Brit, it seemed like Dante really believed everything he was saying. But then, he wasn't at The Floating Eye. Whatever he had heard about The Duels had to have come from Ramses. The version of events Dante heard probably left out the parts about Ramses using a Lamia as one of his champions.

Still, the Paladin's defiant defense of his king was really getting on Brit's nerves. "What?" she said. "Libra should have let others fight for her like Ramses? I guess you live longer being a coward."

"I have heard enough of your insults," Dante snarled. "Send whoever you like to the summit. They should journey south to the Grand Highway's end and keep going. A representative of the king will meet them in the Fens. I guarantee they will be treated with more courtesy than I have been."

"Tell Ramses to expect a representative,"

Hawthorne said politely. "Safe travels on your way back south."

Dante stood with his cape swirling. He was at the door of the kitchen when he stopped and looked back. "I have another message," he said, his voice falling back into its bland courtesy. "For Suzanne."

"For me?" Up until then, Suze had been so quiet Brit almost forgot she was there.

"Yes. The king wished me to inform you that he holds the key to the Oracle Chamber. He said that he would be willing to discuss the terms of a trade if you attend the summit."

Suzanne looked like someone had slapped her in the face.

Dante left the house with his cloak swirling behind him. Hawthorne motioned to the guards to follow him. "See that he doesn't get up to any mischief," the old NPC cautioned them. They moved quickly to catch up to the Paladin.

"How did he know?" Suzanne said.

"Know what?" Mikayla asked.

"How did he know I'm trying to open the Oracle Chamber? Is he spying on us?" Suzanne looked around the kitchen, as if she expected to find one of Ramses's agents hiding under the table.

Brit fought the urge to laugh. "Relax, Suze. One of the Citizens upstairs probably told him. I mean, Mikayla said they hate you guys, so it would make sense if they were reporting on you for Ramses. Isn't that right, Mikayla?"

"I haven't seen any of them spying," Mikayla said.

"So? You're down here half the time."

Suzanne didn't look convinced. Her expression was taut, her eyebrows furrowed with concentration.

Hawthorne shrugged. "I don't know a thing about this key, but we need someone to represent us at the summit," he said. "I don't think these legs of mine will make it down to the Fenlands and back."

Finally, they were going to get to do something! Brit wasn't stoked about mucking through the Fens again, but anything was better than continuing to sit around Zenith City. Brit was about to volunteer them when Mikayla caught Brit's eye and shook her head. Hawthorne saw it; his face fell into a frown.

"We don't have anyone else we can send. Not many could make it to the Fenlands these days, with what Altair's come to."

"I'm sorry," Mikayla said, "but we can't go. Suzanne has to keep working on opening the Oracle Chamber and we can't leave her here alone. Right, Suzanne?"

"Oh," Suzanne said. She looked surprised she was being talked to. "Um, yeah. I guess I need to keep working."

Brit sighed. "It's been ten days."

"So?" Mikayla said.

Brit turned to Suzanne. "Tell me you're close to figuring this out."

"I've got some theories," Suzanne said quietly.

Mikayla didn't argue the point. Instead, she asked, "What about the City Guard? That komodo would have crushed them if we weren't there. How long are they going to last without us?"

Maybe a day, Brit thought. *If that long*. The guards had made some progress but they were a long way away from holding the suburbs themselves.

"Don't worry about the guard," Hawthorne said. "We were dealing with monsters before the three of you came back and that was before you trained us. The guard will manage, but the suburb won't, not without more Energite. Half the lamps in the suburbs are out and how long is it before the elevator stops running? If we're trapped down here when a real horde shows up then it will take more than you three to save us."

"See?" Brit said, even if she wasn't sure

Hawthorne was right. "If he says they'll be fine, they'll be fine."

Mikayla wasn't finished. "You really think it's a good idea to go to this summit? There's like a zero percent chance this isn't some kind of trap."

"And if it is? Do you really think we can't handle it? Besides, I thought you wanted Ramses to answer for all the shit he did."

Mikayla didn't take the bait, but she looked uncertain, which was progress. At least she wasn't refusing outright.

"We should go," Suzanne said. She sounded dejected, depressed even. "I can't open the Oracle Chamber. We need that key."

Brit was shocked to hear Suzanne admit that. She had never expected Suzanne to admit she didn't know what she was doing in Io.

Mikayla rolled her eyes. "I'm sure if we just ask nicely he'll just give it to us."

Brit shrugged. "Who said anything about asking nicely? Look, I want to get Ramses as much as you do. Now we know where to find him. You really think we should just pass on this opportunity?"

Even though Mikayla thought about if for another minute, Brit knew she had won the moment Suzanne had joined her side. Finally, Mikayla sighed and said to Hawthorne, "I'm down. We'll represent you if you're willing to let us."

"I was hoping you'd say that." Hawthorne's craggy face broke out into a smile. "I'll have Henny make you a banner to mark you as our representative."

As they stood to leave, he added, "I know I told Dante to travel safe, but that was just courtesy. I'm really hoping the three of you make it back."

Brit smiled. "Please. We haven't met the monster that can take care of the three of us."

Hawthorne shook his head. "It's not just the monsters I'm worried about."

Outside in the twilight of the suburb, Brit felt a lightness in her chest—no more sitting around twiddling her thumbs. Mikayla looked uncertain and Suzanne still looked kind of dour.

"Don't worry," Brit said. "Whatever he throws at us, you know I've got your back."

"I'm not worried about Ramses," Mikayla said. "Not yet, at least. We're going to have to listen to you complain the entire way across Altair, aren't we?"

Chapter 4

Suzanne was finding it hard to believe she was in Altair. The Grand Highway lay in shambles. Something had taken huge divots out of the road, leaving potholes bigger than Brit for the girls to walk around. The grass spilled over the sides of the road, choking the Grand Highway with weeds.

This didn't look like Altair at all; the overgrown road and wilderness aspect looked way more like Pyxis. Suzanne wondered if Ramses had extended an invitation to the Pyxians as well. Ostensibly, there was now peace between their kingdoms, but Suzanne couldn't imagine the Pyxians would trust Ramses enough to send anyone.

Soon after they got onto the Grand Highway, the girls ran into a merchant, one of the countless buyers and sellers of items the game generated. The NPC greeted the girls pleasantly enough, showing them the average items he carried on his cart. For all the warmth of his greeting, Suzanne couldn't help noticing that both the merchant and his cart had seen better times.

Brit and Mikayla examined his goods, testing out a few of the weapons. Suzanne was interested in selling not buying, so she waited for her friends to finish.

"Do you have any ranged weapons?" Brit asked the merchant. As he brought out more wares, Brit explained, "I'm sick of only having melee attacks."

"Well, you are a Dragoon," Suzanne pointed out. "It's not like you can use a bow."

However, Dragoons could use throwing axes

fine, and luckily the merchant had a decent selection of those. Brit ended up buying them all. The transaction went fine—Brit haggled the merchant's price down a few gold pieces—and easy enough, the axes went into her inventory.

But when Suzanne tried to sell to the merchant everything fell apart. Merchants were supposed to buy anything. That was the one surefire way to convert your loot into gold. Loot from monster kills ranged from animal hides to rare weapons, but Suzanne tended to find animal hides and other rubbish items, which meant she cashed out often. The merchant watched her pull were-monkey hides out of her inventory with growing disdain, until she produced the fifteenth, at which point he pointedly asked, "And what am I supposed to do with this?"

"Buy them?" Suzanne ventured. The merchant snorted in disgust.

"Don't know where you been," he said, "but the whole kingdom's falling apart. Can't even make circuits of the cities anymore on account of there being no one with gold left in them. Who's going to want to buy fifteen weremonkey pelts?"

Suzanne didn't know what to say. Merchants always bought her items. That was how she programmed them. Sometimes they might buy at a lower price than she wanted, but they would always take the dregs of her inventory if she was selling. She had never thought before about what the NPCs actually did with all the crap she unloaded onto them. Did they really resell it all? Suzanne tried to picture NPCs approaching merchants to purchase the vast quantities of pelts, rusty swords, and other garbage she had received while grinding out experience points.

She offered to sell them at half the usual price but the merchant stood firm in his refusal to buy. "We don't have time for this," Brit muttered, so Suzanne was forced to head on with her inventory still full of the useless weremonkey pelts. She ended up ditching them a few miles south.

As they traveled south, the landscape grew less and less familiar. In place of the inns that lined the Grand Highway there were now the skeletons of buildings, often with only one wall remaining. Many places where an inn had stood were now empty lots.

Further away from the Grand Highway, at the end of NPC-made dirt paths, Suzanne saw what looked to be forts. It was getting late in the day, and since there were no other buildings around, the girls decided to take their chances at the nearest fort.

As Suzanne approached the fort, she realized that its main building had been an inn. The fort's wall was made of wood patched together from several different buildings. Suzanne wondered if the fort's occupants had stripped down the nearby inns to build it. The wall would keep out random monsters, she supposed, but it wouldn't do much against anything really dangerous. At the top, the wall wasn't wide enough to man, and it wasn't high enough to discourage climbers. Suzanne saw plenty of grooves and seams between the scavenged wood where she could climb up.

With the sound of creaking chains, the wall's portcullis rose to let out a Fighter. He wore a round shield strapped to his left arm and carried a small mace with his right. His armor was simple mail; Suzanne figured one good attack would split it. Stray curls of brown hair peeked out from beneath his half-helm. All in all, he didn't look anything like a threat to them.

He stopped a few paces away from the girls. "This is Lady Mara's land," the NPC said. "You may not pass without offering my lady tribute."

"Who?" Brit asked, stepping up to him. She towered over the fighter.

He looked up at her, swallowed, and took a step back. "Lady Mara," he said, his voice quavering. "All those who wish to pass must pay tribute to—"

"We heard you the first time," Brit snapped. Suzanne covered her mouth to hide her smile. Mikayla also had to hide her face. Brit would break character if they started laughing. It was hard not to: the Fighter was the funniest thing they had seen since leaving Zenith City.

Brit was on the edge of using the Fighter for a punching bag. Suzanne knew traveling was Brit's least favorite part of the game and Brit was looking to blow off some steam. As flimsy as the fort's defenses looked, starting that fight probably wasn't in the girls' best interests.

"Who is Lady Mara?" Suzanne asked, doing her best to sound courteous.

The Fighter looked uneasily at Brit before answering. "My lady is the ruler of this land, extending from her fort to the Grand Highway and west toward the Ion River." He then rambled for several minutes about the Lady Mara's various virtues, which included her sense of justice, her benevolence, and her impeccable interior design.

Before Brit lost her patience entirely, Suzanne interrupted the Fighter.

"We're new around here. When did your Lady take charge of these lands?"

The Fighter looked down at his shoes. "About a month ago," he muttered.

Considering the fort, that made sense. The building looked like a strong wind might knock it over. Whoever this Mara was, she was richer in subjects than in material wealth.

"We seek an audience with your lady," Mikayla said, effortlessly adopting the courtly speech of the NPCs. "We have traveled all day and would also appreciate the protection her keep might provide."

"My lady is not here at present," the Fighter replied. "She has journeyed south to attend the Fen King's summit. I'm her steward, Joaquin."

Brit yawned and stretched. The steward flinched away from her. "What's to stop us from knocking your door down and taking all your shit?" Brit asked.

"I am," he answered meekly. He raised his mace, but it looked like a baby's rattle next to Brit.

"My friend is joking," Suzanne said hastily. "But it would be great if we could stay here for the night. We could pay you for our beds and a meal if you can spare it." She shot Brit a look; the NPCs were less likely to give them trouble if she would stop scaring them.

The steward hesitated, not sure if he should trust these three high-leveled strangers. Ultimately, either his courtesy or his fear of Brit won out. He shouted a command and the portcullis was raised again. Brit had to duck to fit beneath the gate.

The inside of the fort was, if anything, less impressive than the outside. Within its wooden walls it really was just a reinforced inn. Half a dozen small buildings—little more than huts and lean-tos—crowded the courtyard. The former inn towered over these little dwellings, but it still looked lackluster. Each building had a flagpole affixed to its roof, displaying the same flag: three interlocking azure rings on a white background. Suzanne realized the three blue rings were also stamped on Joaquin's shield.

Like the walls surrounding it, the inn was reinforced with odd bits of wood and metal, attached haphazardly to the preexisting structure. The door of the keep was open, creaking in the light breeze. A Citizen woman exited with a basket of rolls, gave the girls a curious look, and then began to pass out the rolls to the other Citizens. A handful of NPC children were playing tag, darting around the courtyard and generally being underfoot.

Coming closer, Suzanne saw that some of the lean-tos were businesses. An Archer haggled with a merchant over the cost of arrows while a second merchant sold a Citizen a wooden table.

Suzanne was disappointed to see neither of the merchants carried any kind of animal pelts. Next to the spear-seller, small tufts of smoke belched from a forge while its smith hammered the forge spots of a sword.

Suzanne heard an NPC cry out. Reflexively she reached for a dagger but there was no need. On the far side of the courtyard, where the grass was thin and muddy, Citizens were sparring with makeshift spears.

"How do you think they'd do against your guys?" Suzanne asked Brit.

Brit snorted. "They'd all end up stabbing themselves. None of these Citizens are worth shit in a fight."

As she spoke, a red-haired Citizen stabbed at his sparring partner. The other NPC didn't have to defend herself; the red-haired Citizen slipped in mud and fell. His partner hesitated, unsure if she should hit him while he was down or help him back up. She decided on the former course of action, but as she started her coup de grace, her foot skidded out in front of her. She crashed into her sparring partner, leaving both Citizens defeated in the mud.

Brit laughed. "What did I tell you? They're hopeless."

Joaquin cleared his throat. "Begging your pardon, but you are wrong."

Brit gave the Fighter a quizzical look.

"They train because they have hope. Why would they bother otherwise? Citizens do not gain skills in combat like we do but still they try to defend themselves."

There was a loud splattering sound as another NPC toppled into the mud. Joaquin sighed. "I am not saying they fight well, but at least their courage is not lacking."

"It's very brave of them to try,'" Mikayla said. Brit made an impatient little tutting sound, but after that she kept her comments to herself.

Suzanne watched the Citizens with a renewed

interest. Sometimes she forgot that the rest of Io kept going while she wasn't around. She wondered how many monster attacks the Citizens suffered before they decided to fight back. She knew Brit was working on something similar with the Zenith Citizens, but Brit's Citizens were little more than a glorified alarm system. She knew Brit and Mikayla handled all of the real fighting. But who could these Citizens call on when they were outmatched?

"Who's in charge of their training?" she asked Joaquin.

He flushed. "I am. Lady Mara saw to their training before she departed. With her gone, I am all that is left." Joaquin shook his head. He looked as if his position made him miserable. Suzanne could understand that. Even though he was an NPC with a class, Joaquin didn't look that tough. He was still holding his shield and mace like he was afraid they would disappear if he let them go.

"She spearheaded our defenses. My lady is a formidable warrior and a patient instructor. I am a poor replacement."

Suzanne could see Mikayla's breaking heart writ large upon her face. *We don't have time to help every NPC we meet*, she thought. *Every minute we waste on the road is that much longer before we get home.*

Joaquin seemed to shake off his moment of doubt. "Follow me inside," he said. "I will find you suitable accommodations."

Chapter 5

Brit's eyes snapped open. In that first moment after waking, the ceiling was foreign to her, the room strange. *You're in that fort*, she told herself. *You're fine.*

Her heart was racing. She tried to remember what she had been dreaming and felt the dream slipping through her fingers. She had been in a dungeon again. Ramses was there, being the smug shithead he always was. And Suzanne had been in the dream, but it wasn't really Suzanne? The Suzanne-not-Suzanne was attacking someone, but who? She couldn't remember.

It was just a dream, she told herself. She leaned

back into the bed and closed her eyes, waiting for unconsciousness. Sleep did not come.

She tried rolling over onto her shoulder, looking for some way to lie comfortably on the stereotypically hard NPC bed. Normally all she had to do to fall asleep in the game was close her eyes while lying down, but it wasn't happening. *Just another glitch in the game.* After a few more minutes tossing and turning, she gave up and got out of bed.

The NPCs who fortified the inn didn't bother barricading the windows on the second floor. Brit watched the courtyard, illuminated by a full moon. Brit could see Mara's flag fluttering on the roof of each building, the three blue rings brilliant in the moonlight. A couple of Citizens patrolled the interior of the wall. But what good would that do? They wouldn't see an enemy coming until they had crested that wall, and at that point, a few Citizens with wooden spears wouldn't be able to stop any serious threats. Did it make them feel safe? She didn't know. Brit spent little time worrying about NPCs' feelings.

She turned from the window. Mikayla and Suze were both still asleep in their beds, their features frozen. Brit wondered if that was how she looked while she slept. She almost laughed—she didn't even know what she looked like in Io. There were no mirrors in the game, so besides catching a glimpse in a still body of water, she had never seen her character. Now that she thought about it, not knowing was kind of freeing.

Asleep, her friends looked like her friends. Suzanne's eyebrows were furrowed, like how they got whenever she heard something in the game wasn't working right. *Well, something isn't working right. I can't get back to sleep.*

Mikayla was sleeping on top of her covers, dressed in light armor. Her swords were in her inventory. Brit had noticed that Mikayla only took them off now when she was sleeping. *What's she so worried about?* Brit wondered. Mikayla looked peaceful. Like nothing in the world could hurt her. Maybe she was dreaming, too: about the real world and going home. Not for the first time, Brit considered waking Mikayla up and confessing all the weird dreams she'd been having. But after a moment that fancy passed.

Even while they slept in stasis, the little green icons marking them as player characters floated next to Suzanne and Mikayla's heads. Brit looked up, half-expecting to see her own icon, but she knew it wasn't there. That made sense, after all. The girls knew who they were and where they came from, even if the NPCs didn't.

She was getting restless. If she wasn't going to sleep, then it didn't make sense to stand around in the dark, not with so many hours until morning. The floorboards creaked beneath her feet as she crossed the room to the door. She forgot to duck under the doorway and smacked her head on the frame.

"Fuck," she hissed. She thought she heard

someone stirring behind her, but when she turned to check both Suze and Mikayla still seemed to be asleep. Making sure she ducked this time, she stepped out of the room into the hallway.

Downstairs all the windows were barricaded, leaving the common room of the inn almost completely dark. She waited at the foot of the stairs while her eyes adjusted. After a few moments she could make out a figure slumped over at one of the tables. Upon closer inspection, she discovered it was Joaquin. The Fighter lay on his arms, snoring lightly. It was funny—sleeping Joaquin looked far more alive than either of her frozen friends upstairs. She left him where he was and tiptoed out the front door.

The Citizens on guard duty stopped when they saw her emerge from the inn. She gave them half a wave and crossed the courtyard to join them.

"How's it going?" she asked.

"Fine," one of them answered. Her spear reached up to Brit's chin but the Citizen herself barely reached Brit's belly button. Yet she didn't balk from Brit like Joaquin had.

"I couldn't sleep," Brit said. "Is it cool if I do patrol with you?"

The short spearwoman nodded. Patrol, it turned out, really was just the NPCs making circuits of the courtyard. After three times around, Brit couldn't help herself.

"You should really check outside the walls," she said. "You already know there's no one in here."

"There could be monsters outside," a balding NPC said. He shuddered. "What are we going to do if one attacks?" The other guards nodded in uneasy agreement.

Fight it, dumbass. But Brit couldn't tell him that. She had never experienced Io as a Citizen. All the monsters she plowed through must be beyond terrifying to them. "Don't worry," she told them. "I'll be with you. I can handle anything that shows up, or at least distract it long enough for you to get back inside."

She took a step toward the portcullis. None of them followed her. "Come on," she said. "I bet there's nothing even out there."

The balding guard muttered disagreement. "Fine," Brit said. "At least lift the gate so I can take a look around."

That much they were glad to do, though Brit had to wonder if they were just happy to get rid of her. The portcullis rattled open. Brit crossed through into the outside world.

"Wait!" she heard. Turning back she saw the short spearwoman jogging over to her. "You should not be out there without backup," she said.

And you're my backup? Still, it made Brit feel better that at least one of the guards was willing to come with her. At least one of them had the nerve. Outside, the walls were just as calm as within. Off in the distance, Brit could see the shadows of monsters moving, but whatever creatures were out there didn't make any moves toward the inn. The grass grew high this far off the Grand Highway, but the NPCs had cleared a perimeter around the inn. Otherwise her Citizen partner would have been swallowed by the field.

"They call me Gwynedd," the NPC said. "You are Brit, correct? I overheard you and your companions introducing yourselves to Joaquin."

"Yeah, I'm Brit." They walked in silence for a few steps. Reaching the end of the western wall, they turned and continued following the wall east.

"You are right," Gwynedd said suddenly. "We cannot afford to be afraid. Without Lady Mara, we have let ourselves become like children. Even if we do not have classes we must fight."

Brit was taken aback. She had no idea her feelings were so transparent to the NPCs. "Joaquin said he was training you."

Gwynedd shook her head. "If you can call

it training. We need to be out here fighting against real monsters. We cannot just hide inside anymore."

Gwynedd stopped and thrust her spear angrily into the ground. "I will not forget the day the wards failed. My village was unprotected. When the first creature crossed the threshold we thought it was some illusion, some trick. But then another followed and another. Before we could send for help we were overrun."

"I'm sorry." The apology felt hollow but Brit didn't know what else to say.

"I hid. That was how I survived. And now I hide still. It does not matter who puts a weapon in my hand. Why is it that some are strong and others are weak?"

Maybe it would have been better to do this alone, Brit thought. She pulled Gwynedd's spear out of the earth and handed it back to her. The NPC hesitated and then took it. They resumed the circuit—Brit in front and Gwynedd behind her—neither speaking until they reached the southern wall's end and turned north.

"I do not mean to burden you with my troubles," the Gwynedd said. "But you and your companions walk the Grand Highway without fear, like the wards still worked. If I had your strength I would not need to hide."

"We're still spending the night behind your walls," Brit called back to her. "We still take damage. We're just a little better at dishing it out, that's all."

"Still, if I had a fraction—" A sputtering sound replaced Gwynedd's words. Brit turned to see the point of an arrow protruding from the Citizen's neck. Gwynedd fell forward, collapsing into pixels as she hit the earth.

She didn't wait to see who had loosed the shaft. Sprinting back to the portcullis, Brit shouted, "Lift the fucking gate! We're under attack!"

The portcullis remained shut. "Let me in!"

Brit yelled. Through the portcullis she could see the other NPCs retreating back into the inn.

Brit didn't have time to be pissed off. She squatted and grabbed hold of the portcullis. Grunting, she threw all her strength into lifting. She managed to raise it up to her chest, just high enough for her to duck under. The portcullis slammed shut behind her, but it didn't matter. They were coming over the walls.

Three Rogues dropped down over the makeshift barricade. They pulled their black cloaks back to reveal belts of knives, just like Suzanne's. Brit didn't have time to equip her halberd. She grabbed the nearest NPC and threw him at the others. The other Rogues ducked their colleague. The one Brit had thrown hit the wall with a crunch and didn't get back up.

But there were more than just those three. Rogues dropped down from all sides—seven more in total. Brit could see the moonlight reflected off the blades of their daggers and the heads of their arrows.

The door of the inn kicked open. Joaquin took a few confused steps outside and was immediately engaged by two of the Rogues. They drove him away from the door and three of the Rogues raced inside.

Brit ran toward the inn, but one of the Rogues threw himself at her. She grabbed him out of the air and slammed him into the ground, stomping on his chest with all her weight just to make sure he stayed there.

She heard the sound of fighting coming from inside the inn. An NPC screamed and then Mikayla appeared in the doorway, one of her swords embedded in a Rogue up to the hilt. She pulled the blade out and raced over to Brit.

"Where's Suzanne?"

Mikayla nodded to the roof of the inn. A shadow crawled over the thatched roof. It fell on one of the Rogues fighting Joaquin, landed lightly, and then sprang at the Fighter's other assailant.

"More are headed toward the inn!" Suzanne shouted as her second target exploded into pixels. Brit saw them. She grabbed her halberd out of her inventory and ran toward the inn's door. The last Rogue in pulled the door shut behind him. Brit reached the inn, grabbed the door knob, and the entire building exploded into flames.

She threw her arms up to cover her face. The explosion sent her flying back into the courtyard. When she got up, the world within the walls had become fire and chaos. The Citizens inside the inn cried for help and steel clashed against steel as Suzanne, Mikayla, and Joaquin engaged the other Rogues.

Brit saw a Rogue slip past Joaquin's shield and land a backstab on the Fighter. He went down on one knee, swinging his mace wildly as the Rogue dodged backwards. "Help them!" he cried. "They're trapped in the inn!"

"Cover Joaquin!" Brit shouted to no one, to everyone. She lowered her shoulder and smashed through the front door. The Rogues must have used Naphtha Bombs; the air was thick with smoke and the flames were everywhere. The walls creaked and groaned, brittle from the heat. Brit didn't know how long they were going to hold.

Where did the Citizens go? Covering her mouth with her free hand, Brit fought through the flames to the bottom of the stairs. She took three steps up before the stairs fell out, crumbling to pixels beneath her feet. She landed hard on her stomach as debris rained down on top of her. Half-buried, she felt the flames lick at her and saw her health bar dropping. The exit was lost behind a wall of smoke and ash.

She began to flail in her panic. She grabbed for something, anything with which to pull herself out of the rubble. Her hands scrabbled over the floor, finding the corner of the collapsed stair-case. She pulled so hard her muscles felt like they were on fire, but she didn't dare stop. Finally, she broke free of the pile of rubble and staggered to the wall.

There was no door on this wall, so she made one. She reached into her inventory and grabbed her halberd. Three quick strikes and the wall opened out into the courtyard again. Brit tumbled out of the smoke and lay panting on the grass.

She breathed hard, sharp breaths. The clean air felt like a knife in her lungs, but it was also sweeter than anything she had ever tasted. Her whole body shuddered with every breath. She couldn't remember ever feeling so exhausted before in her life.

"It's going to collapse!" she heard someone shout. Brit felt hands grab her shoulders and let herself be dragged. The last supporting wall of the inn gave way and the whole building collapsed in on itself, spitting out a cloud of ash and pixels. The three-ringed flag fluttered down to the ground, caught flame and was destroyed.

"Who?" Brit asked weakly.

"You dumbass!" Mikayla shouted. "What the fuck were you thinking? Couldn't you see the whole thing was going to come down?"

"Joaquin . . . " Brit muttered. She took a deep breath and tried to steady herself. Joaquin had said to help the Citizens in the inn, but where were they? And where was he? Looking around the courtyard Brit saw the Rogues were gone. Suzanne was stooped over a small treasure chest, grabbing the loot left after the battle. Brit almost called out to her, to ask who she was looting. Not that it mattered. Regardless of who had won the battle, all of the NPCs had lost.

Mikayla stood over Brit, her hands on her hips, her expression a cross between anger and worry.

They're all dead, Brit realized. *Either the flames got them or they went when the building did.*

"Are you okay?" she asked Mikayla.

"I'm fine. So's Suzanne. But what about you? You can't even stand up."

Brit chose to ignore that. "Was I the only one who got out?"

"Yeah," Mikayla answered, shaking her head. "What an absolute mess."

"I'd say so."

Brit recognized that voice. She turned and saw, perched atop the wall, Gemini. The Assassin's long black cloak covered her entire body, except for her head, which was wrapped in a featureless mask. But Brit didn't need to see her face to know that Gemini was gloating. Gemini was the NPC who beat Suzanne on The Floating Eye, and she'd taunted Suzanne throughout the fight.

"Imagine this. The three of you show up at an inn. They're in dire straits. Monsters attacking left and right and their lady and protector has gone to the Fens for a summit. Bandits attack and the three brave heroes rush to defend the poor, defenseless Citizens."

Gemini laughed softly. She vaulted off the wall and landed gracefully in the ruined courtyard. "Except the heroes don't save them. The heroes watch them die and can't do anything about it."

"What are you doing here?" Suzanne demanded.

"I can't imagine why he wants you alive," the Assassin continued, ignoring Suzanne.

"I asked what you were doing here." Brit saw the dagger in Suzanne's hand and heard the anger in her voice.

The Assassin laughed again. "It was supposed to be a test. Which you all failed, I might add." She spread her arms wide in a mocking shrug. "Besides, I missed you. Without the three of you things just haven't been as much fun. Especially you, Suzanne. Haven't you been dying for a rematch?"

Suzanne answered by slinging her dagger at Gemini's head. The Assassin ducked. The dagger clattered off the wall behind her. Suzanne was already charging across the courtyard. Mikayla ran at an angle, forming a pincer. Gemini couldn't go left or right and behind her was the wall.

But the Assassin hardly seemed concerned. "So you missed me too!" she crowed. "Don't worry, we'll be seeing a lot more of each other soon."

Suzanne was two paces away. Gemini swung her cape up. The black material swirled over her face. Brit saw three capsules drop out from the cape. When they hit the ground, the capsules exploded into a cloud of smoke. By the time it cleared, Gemini was gone.

"Where did she go?" Suzanne shouted. "Where is she?"

"She disappeared," Mikayla said. She thrust one of her swords into the ground. Brit was reminded of Gwynedd doing the same with her spear only a few hours earlier. Now she was gone, with the rest of the NPCs from the inn.

"Do you think she brought those Rogues?" Brit asked.

"Who else could it have been?" Suzanne snapped. "Of course it was her."

The anger in Suzanne's voice surprised Brit. But, she mused, she shouldn't have been so surprised. It was Gemini who beat Suzanne during The Duels on The Floating Eye. Suzanne wasn't going to let that go so easily. But Brit didn't care about Suzanne's grudges right now. She wanted to sleep. Maybe when she woke up, this would all have been another dream. The inn would still be standing and the Citizens would be sparring in the courtyard, training for a fight that hadn't happened yet. All it took was a look at Suzanne and Mikayla's faces to know that wasn't the case.

Mikayla rooted through the rubble and managed to find a singed cot. Brit fell onto it and into a dreamless sleep. When dawn broke they left the inn, collapsed and smoldering. They trekked through the overgrowth to the Grand Highway. Brit didn't look back.

Chapter 6

You can fix it once you get home. Suzanne repeated the words in her head the rest of the journey down to the Fenlands. They were her first thought when she rose in the morning and her last thought before she slept at night. Ever since she found out she was trapped in Io, Suzanne had been compiling a list of all the gameplay features that weren't working right. That was her to-do list, what she'd focus on fixing as soon as she made it home.

After the inn the words took on a different meaning. She was no longer sure what *it* was. Was *it* the inconsistent XP system? The wards around towns and cities? Or was their something wrong on a deeper level, corrupting the rest of the virtual world? Every time Suzanne thought she had figured out all the glitches she found another one to add to her list.

Whatever *it* was, Suzanne could fix it as soon as she was back in the real world. Of course, if that was her goal, then she was walking the wrong direction. The Oracle Chamber was back in Zenith City and with each passing day the girls traveled farther and farther away from the Altairi capital.

Suzanne kept her thoughts to herself. They traveled most of the way in silence, each girl occupied with her own thoughts. Suzanne tried her hardest to focus on her list of glitches and to ignore her memories of the inn and the fire. But sometimes, unbidden, her mind turned to Gemini. It was the way Gemini had taunted her that Suzanne fixated on; something about her felt so different from the other NPCs working for

Ramses. Ramses's other henchmen—like Burgrave, for example—were unflinching in their loyalty to the king, but they fought for duty. Gemini was more like one of the bitchy girls from Suzanne's school; she drew genuine enjoyment from her actions. Suzanne couldn't get the image of the Assassin laughing as the inn burned with the NPCs trapped inside out of her head.

Gemini said the inn had been a test, but who was she testing them for? Ramses? Herself? And how had Gemini found them? There'd been no sign of the Assassin on the Grand Highway, but as soon as they let their guard down Gemini showed up. All Suzanne knew for sure was that the next time she ran into Gemini, the Assassin wasn't getting away without giving up some answers.

The girls steered clear of all the settlements they saw. Mikayla scouted out the towns closest to the Highway and found they were all deserted. They saw forts and compounds like Lady Mara's, but none of them suggested leaving the Grand Highway. In fact, none of the girls talked much at all. Mikayla was gone half the time scouting ahead, and when she did travel with Brit and Suzanne she would only talk about what she had scouted. Brit was no better. She abandoned her usual joking bullshit and marched down the Grand Highway with a determination that made Suzanne uncomfortable.

Early some mornings before they set out, Suzanne saw Brit and Mikayla speaking quietly by themselves. Ever since the girls came back to Zenith City, Suzanne had sensed that her friends were talking, if not behind her back, then intentionally away from her. She figured they were probably talking about her. Well, that was fine. Even if she wasn't their subject, then they must have been discussing what had happened at the inn, or in Pyxis, and Suzanne didn't want to talk about either of those things. All she wanted to do was get to the Fenlands for this stupid summit and leave as soon as possible.

The only monsters they saw were in the distance, indistinct shapes on the horizon. Mikayla reported the same from her scouting excursions. Most likely they were so high-level the monsters stayed away. She would have loved the chance to study the monsters, to see if they had changed like the rest of Altair. Suzanne would have welcomed the distraction from her own thoughts.

Because they were avoiding inns, they slept in small copses or in open fields under the stars, or they didn't sleep at all and kept on going straight through the night. Brit set the pace, her long strides swallowing the Grand Highway.

Four days after leaving the inn the ground softened and the trees grew thicker. They had reached the outskirts of the Fenlands. Suzanne was exhausted from their sprint south and was aching for a bed, even one of the hard NPC cots. But if anything, Brit sped up now that their destination was in sight. Dante had said to head south past the highway's end, promising that someone would meet them in the Fenlands. Another day of traveling and they reached the Fenlands proper. Suzanne's excitement over seeing this area of the map evaporated roughly ten seconds after entering it.

The Grand Highway ran into a pool of quicksand and didn't come out on the other side. The sun disappeared as well, hidden behind an impermeable canopy of trees. Constant dusk was their companion in the new kingdom of Ramses. Suzanne had no idea how anyone would be able to find them in the murky Fenlands. She began to wonder if the whole summit was just some stupid prank of Ramses's, designed to draw them out and leave Zenith City unprotected.

But at that point, Suzanne didn't really care what Ramses was plotting. She was too busy yelling at herself for ever thinking the Fenlands would be a good idea for a game environment.

Suzanne and Mikayla were fine with the change in terrain, but in her armor Brit was so heavy she would sink into the loamy earth. Similarly, Suzanne could squeeze between the dense forest, but Brit had to knock trees out of her way or find a wider path to go down. They had traveled to the Fenlands in silence, but now that they were in the Fens the air rang with monsters hooting and howling and Brit cursing all the trees, vines, quicksand, and swamps in Altair.

"Fuck this!" Brit shouted. She had sunk ankle-deep into a bog. They had to stop while she got herself free. The bog was unwilling to release her. There was a loud pop as she yanked her foot out. Her boot had filled with slime and made squelching noises. That just gave Brit another opportunity to complain, which she took with a passion.

"This is such bullshit!" *Squelch*. "Who holds a summit in the middle of a fucking swamp?"

Squish, squish. "Where the fuck are we even going?" Brit's boot made a noise like a loud fart.

Suzanne couldn't help herself. She covered her mouth to cover her giggles. Brit still heard her and turned to shout at Suzanne, but Mikayla broke down and started laughing too. The anger on Brit's face melted into resignation as she also chuckled.

"If you unequip and re-equip your boot that should get the gunk out," Suzanne told her.

Brit grabbed her halberd. With a single swing she chopped down a tree, knocking it over for a bench. The wood creaked beneath her as she sat on it but the trunk held. Suzanne watched her navigate through her Menu, taking the boot off and putting it back on. Brit tried a few experimental stomps and the squelching noise was indeed gone.

That settled, they headed out again. Mikayla led the way deeper into the swamp, cutting a path with her swords. Suzanne followed behind her with Brit taking the rear.

"Thanks," Suzanne heard Brit say from behind her. "Sorry I've been complaining so much."

Suzanne cut down a vine before answering. "If anyone should apologize it should be me. Seriously, I don't know why I thought the Fenlands would be a good idea." She paused to vault over a mossy log. Suzanne turned back to see Brit taking the more direct approach and just throwing the log out of her way.

"Someone up ahead," Mikayla called back. She drew her other sword and stepped onto a patch of firmer ground, crouching behind an overgrown fern. Suzanne followed her up onto the embankment. Brit struggled after them. If it came to a fight in the Fens, Suzanne thought, then Brit wouldn't have any mobility. But hopefully it wouldn't come to that.

The swamp shadows played tricks on Suzanne's eyes; they shifted and swirled together, making it hard for her to see at any distance. She couldn't make out the figure approaching them through the undergrowth. But she could hear the soft footsteps of the approaching NPC. A familiar voice rang out through the Fens. "I am here to escort the representatives from Zenith City to Fenhold. I assure you I am unarmed."

"Burgrave," Mikayla whispered. Suzanne let out her breath. Even if he served Ramses, she knew that Burgrave was an NPC who kept his word. If he said he was unarmed then he would definitely not be attacking them.

"We're the representatives," Suzanne said, stepping out from behind the plant. Burgrave was a short NPC, completely bald. He favored the fluid robes of the Pyxians over standard Altairi armor. As always, two rubies on silver chains dangled from his ears. They swished as he stopped and regarded Suzanne. If he was surprised that she was the representative, he gave no sign, but Burgrave hardly ever let what he was feeling show on his face.

"I suspected it might be you three," he said politely. "I can see Brit sticking out from behind the fern."

"Hiding's not really my thing," Brit said, standing up. She regarded Burgrave coolly. The NPC offered her the same bland expression in return.

"I should say not. But there seems to be one of you missing. Where is Mikayla?"

"She's right here . . . " Brit's voice trailed off as she ducked behind the fern. She emerged a second later. "Where the hell did she go?"

"I'm over here." Brit, Suzanne, and Burgrave all turned to see Mikayla standing further down the path Burgrave had come up. Suzanne suspected Mikayla was trying to get the drop on Burgrave. They had fought each other on The Floating Eye—Mikayla fighting for Pyxis, Burgrave for Ramses. Despite that, Suzanne didn't sense any animosity between the two of them. If anything, Burgrave was even more polite to Mikayla than he had been to Brit and Suzanne.

The path he led them on wound through the Fenlands. At times, Suzanne thought they were doubling back and covering the same ground twice. But she also saw that Brit was having a much easier time of it: the ground could better support her size, and the trees grew wider apart, making it easier for them all to follow Burgrave's bald head through the swamp.

The trees began to thin out and the path widened until there were no longer any vines to duck under or overgrowth to sidestep. The way cleared so gradually that Suzanne didn't notice it until they stepped into a vast clearing. Here the trees grew so tall that their dark canopy was like a second sky. The sunlight that wormed its way through took the place of stars. It was beneath the false stars that Suzanne first saw Ramses's new castle, Fenhold.

She thought back to the makeshift keep at Lady Mara's inn. Compared to Fenhold, it looked like a merchant's stall. Fenhold was encircled by a black stone wall dozens of feet high. A battlement wrapped around the top of the wall, manned by NPCs in black armor. Even from the ground, Suzanne could make out the sigil on their armor: the crimson four-pillared insignia that was plastered all over Zenith City. *You can take the king off of his pillars*, she mused, *but he'll still put himself up on a pedestal.*

The only break she could see in the black walls was a massive gate, its steel bars biting into the earth like fangs. Rising above the battlements was Fenhold's single tower. Suzanne could see lights flickering in the tower's windows. *Had this always been here?* She had never designed a castle like this. The Fens were supposed to be a dungeon meant to be cleared by the players. When and how had the NPCs managed to construct Fenhold here in the middle of a swamp?

Burgrave led the girls to the gate, where a procession of NPCs were entering the castle. "I must return to my station in the Fens. There are others to be escorted," he explained, bowing solemnly. "When King Ramses chose this location for his castle I do not believe he expected to receive so many visitors."

Suzanne watched him disappear back into the swamp, glad at least to be staying on solid ground. She didn't recognize any of the NPCs she waited behind, but from the finery of their dress and the number of advanced class characters present among them, she guessed they must be nobility from the rest of Altair. Many of them were Citizens. She supposed Ramses was a Citizen as well, as she had never made a class specifically for nobility. But alongside the Citizen nobles were classed NPCs. Mostly melee classes, like Paladins and Defenders, with the odd Ranger sprinkled in. No Archers, no Rogues. Suzanne wondered if certain classes were more disposed to claiming nobility. Maybe classes that took more damage—like Paladins, or Monks—were prone to the needs of others above their own. Or maybe they were the NPCs most likely to seize power.

Leading the procession were two of Ramses's Paladins. The crowd moved quickly enough, and before long Suzanne was following them through Fenhold's gate. While she was beneath the wall, Suzanne couldn't shake the feeling that the castle was swallowing her whole. The castle's walls were so thick that it took her a solid minute to cross through into the courtyard.

They followed the train of NPCs through the courtyard and into the castle itself. Small windows, right beneath the vaulted ceiling, let in what little light they could, augmented by a scattering of chandeliers. Besides mosaic renditions of Altair's insignia no decorations covered the walls. The NPCs shuffled along, their footsteps loud on the stone floor, but the enormity of the halls muted the sound.

Down one hallway, then another. To Suzanne it felt like they were being led in a spiral inwards, deeper and deeper into Fenhold. *There has to be a faster way through*, she thought. *Ramses just wants to show off his palace.*

As if on cue, the Paladins came to a halt in front of a massive set of doors, much like the one to the throne room in Zenith City. They each grabbed a door and pulled them back to reveal the audience chamber of the king. The NPCs filed in, followed by the girls.

Suzanne's first thought upon entering was that the king had stepped up his security detail. Behind a row of Defenders and Dragoons, standing atop a dais, was Ramses. His thin, pale face contrasted with his wild eyes. Suzanne saw them searching the crowd before him. When they fell upon her, the King's lips curled into a smile.

"Look!" Mikayla whispered.

Suzanne was so intent on watching the king she had failed to notice the other NPCs on the dais. By the king's right hand was Xenos, his hood pulled low over his face as usual. Xenos had been another of Altair's champions during the arena duels. He had defeated Leo with a single attack; what that attack was is as much a mystery as everything else about the NPC. Xenos turned and whispered something into Ramses's ear, who nodded, the smile on his face growing wider.

To the king's left stood Gemini. Suzanne felt a surge of disgust as she regarded the masked Assassin. She had promised she'd be seeing the girls soon, and sure enough, here she was. Suzanne would've liked nothing more than to march up to her, rip the mask off her face and beat her down with it, but she knew she couldn't start something here. Even if the other Altairi were on her side—and she couldn't count on that—there were still the Defenders and Dragoons guarding the front of the dais. Besides, Suzanne had no way of knowing how many soldiers Ramses had stashed in the rest of the castle. Like the rest of

Fenhold, the windows were right beneath the vaulted ceilings, filling the corners of the room with shadows.

The doors swung open, admitting another NPC. Though he was old, the Monk walked gracefully toward the girls. The sleeves of his Pyxian robe were rolled up, revealing burly muscles from long days of working a forge.

"Figured the three of you would find your way here," he said.

"Rigel!" Suzanne hugged the old Monk. "What are you doing here?"

"Same as you, I figure," he replied. "Ramses sent that lapdog of his to New Pyxia. Something about a new spirit of friendship between nations. Leo—King Leo, that is—asked me to come on his behalf, speak for the kingdom. Waste of time, if you ask me. Ramses isn't the kind of friend any of us need."

Brit laughed. "How are things in Pyxis?"

"Hard to say with so much changing so fast.

I'm guessing they'll be done with New Pyxia by the time I get back from this nonsense. The people are coming down from the hills and back from the wandering camps."

He looked directly at Suzanne. "You're all invited to New Pyxia, by the way. I was supposed to tell you if I ran into you. Leo says you've all got a place at his court if you'd like it."

Suzanne looked away. It was easy enough to forget about Pyxis while she stayed in Zenith City, but talking to Rigel made it all come back to her. Her whatever-it-was with Leo felt like it was behind her, but if she was understanding what Rigel said, the new king of Pyxis didn't feel the same. Suzanne was surprised to see Mikayla also looking away uncomfortably. *Mikayla loved Pyxis. I wouldn't be surprised if she went to visit after we were done here.*

"That'd be great," Brit began. Before she could say anything else, the Defenders and Dragoons banged their weapons on the floor, silencing the conversations in the crowd. They all turned to the dais as the king stepped forward to speak.

"My fellow Altairi," the king drawled. "I welcome you all in the spirit of friendship!"

"What did I tell you," Rigel muttered. Ramses was too far away to hear.

"I thank you for making the journey to my new home. I must admit, I had some concerns about the state of our old capital, but I have heard Zenith City is ably defended by its own Citizens. In such hard times, their courage can inspire us all."

He paused as if overcome by emotion. It would have been more effective if he wasn't smirking. "For too long," the king continued. "We have squabbled over our possessions, guarding ours jealously, and coveting our neighbors. But I say no more. What does it matter if this Energite cache was found in the Fenlands? Yes, we found the Energite in the Fens, but the Fens are in

Altair, and Altair is but a part of Io. Does not the Energite then belong to all of us?"

"I say yes. But while we might all have need of Energite our needs do not equal each other. Thus I have called for this summit so that we may justly distribute the Energite to best suit not our needs, but the needs of our world."

The doors opened again and Citizens, dressed as pages with Ramses's sigil as a badge, entered. "We have much to discuss on the morrow. Take this night to rest and refresh yourselves. Tomorrow, our new era of friendship begins!"

Ramses stepped off the dais, followed by Xenos and Gemini. The Dragoons and Defenders formed up around the three of them and pushed through the crowd toward the doors. As she passed the girls, Gemini turned and waved. Brit flipped her off.

One of the pages approached Suzanne. Bowing courteously, he said, "If you would follow me," and started toward the doors.

"Hold a minute," Rigel called. "Leo sent me

with half his guard. I'll send someone to watch you tonight, but you can never have too many eyes open."

Like I need to be told that. The other Pyxians had been waiting in the hall. Rigel spoke to them and a few broke off to follow the girls. As the page led them through the castle, Suzanne did her best to remember the route they took so she could find her way back to the audience chamber later. It was difficult to tell one black stone hallway from another.

Finally, the page came to a stop in front of the staircase. The rooms Ramses gave them were near the top of Fenhold's tower, an arduous climb up. When they finally reached the top, Brit joked, "Ramses is probably hoping we fall down the stairs and break our necks."

Suzanne didn't laugh. She looked around the room, but besides the door and a window there didn't seem to be anyway in or out. It looked safe, or at least as safe as anywhere in Ramses's castle could be.

"Time to get some sleep," Suzanne said. They had been traveling nonstop and tomorrow they needed to be as alert as possible to deal with whatever Ramses had planned for them. She face-planted into bed and fell instantly asleep.

Chapter 7

"**S**ince the war, our forges have not been relit," Talleyrand said. Rolls of fat jiggled beneath the NPC's chin as he spoke. He was attending on behalf of Hobston, a city to the north of Zenith City, nearer the Ion River. Mikayla had met the NPC when the summit convened that morning. She watched him strut back and forth as he spoke and stifled a yawn. Who would have thought the summit would be this boring?

The summit convened early in the morning. Now, the sun was setting and they were no closer to any agreement over the Energite.

Every representative who spoke claimed their constituents needed the Energite the most. If they were to be believed, all of Altair teetered on the brink.

And are they wrong? Mikayla remembered the shape of the Grand Highway as they headed south. Even if this cache of Energite was as big as Ramses said, it might not be enough.

While in Pyxis, Mikayla had taken the availability of Energite for granted. She had forgotten that the Altairi had suffered a shortage of Energite even before the war made them put all of their surplus into forging. Ramses was responsible for the shortage, of course, but in Fenhold the king was essentially untouchable.

He'll get his one day, she thought. That would have to wait until the rest of Altair got its Energite. For now, the NPCs were bound to their former king by their need for the resource.

Ramses sat at the head of the long table, Xenos at his right hand, Burgrave at his left. Gemini was nowhere to be seen; Mikayla wondered what the Assassin was up to. There wasn't much else to do besides listen to the blustering of NPCs like Talleyrand, and Mikayla had had her fill of that shortly after the discussions started. She had been half-listening since then, staring out the stained-glass window that filled half the exterior wall, her frustration building as the NPCs alternated praising Ramses and begging for the biggest piece of the pie. The window was decorated, like seemingly everything else Ramses owned, with Altair's sigil. Mikayla wondered if Ramses was really that egotistical or if he just didn't know any other designs.

Calling it a long table was a bit of an understatement. The room was as long as a hall in Zenith Castle, longer than some of the valleys through which the girls had traveled. The table had to be that long to seat the delegates. Mikayla never imagined there were so many villages and municipalities in Altair. But apparently more were popping up all the time, and each had a delegate clamoring to be heard.

Either the acoustics of the room or some quirk of Io allowed the NPCs to speak audibly without shouting. That was both a blessing and a curse, as it made their speeches that much harder for Mikayla to tune out.

She tuned back in to hear Talleyrand saying, "Pyxian saboteurs extinguished our forges."

"Now, now," Ramses interjected. "You must not forget that our nations were embroiled in a war. Any actions taken by the Pyxians," he paused, and smiled widely at Mikayla and her friends, "or by their agents, has been excused under the terms of our peace. Please, Talleyrand, continue."

The hefty NPC nodded, wobbling. "Yes, your grace. As I was saying, without our forges, Hobston has been reduced from a blazing glory to little more than a cinder. We need this Energite for our commerce. To rekindle our bright flame!"

He beamed down the long table. Clearly he had expected his speech to earn more adulation than it received. *Fat chance*, Mikayla thought. *Not when everybody wants the same damn thing.*

"Thank you," Ramses said, clapping softly as he rose. Talleyrand bowed deeply and waddled back to his seat. "I believe it is past time we heard from Zenith City's representatives. Tell me, Lady Mikayla, how things fare in the Capital."

Mikayla was surprised Ramses called on her. So far he had seemed content to ignore the girls.

"Poorly," she answered. "The lights are going out in the suburbs and the ward has failed. Monsters are slaughtering the Citizens."

"I did not ask of the suburb," Ramses said, his smirk never faltering. "What of the city itself? I hope the fountains of my old home are still leaping."

Mikayla couldn't believe it. "Fountains? Seriously? You abandoned the city, Ramses, taking your whole army with you. You condemned every Citizen in the suburbs and you're asking me about fountains?"

"I had received word that forces from Pyxian had crossed into Altair," came Ramses's flip reply. "Fearing a renewed conflict I sought refuge in the naturally defended Fenlands. Little did I know the reports referred to the three of you. Had I known, then perhaps I would have remained on my throne."

"It's a real shame you didn't," Mikayla snapped. "Considering how Altair really flourished under your leadership."

"Why did you return to Altair?" Ramses's voice was deadly cold now, abandoning the sham friendliness he had spoken with only moments earlier. "I would think Pyxis a better home for three such as you."

"Meaning what exactly?" Rigel asked. He was seated across from the girls. He had been silent all day, but every time Mikayla looked his way he was watching the proceedings with an acute attention, hanging on to every word.

"I assure you no offense is intended," Ramses replied in his usual, mocking voice. "Only that, considering their criminal status, and after rising so high within your military, the representatives from Zenith City might have wished to stay. It was the three of you who led the raids on Altair during the war, if I am not mistaken."

Mikayla judged from the muttering that broke out around the table that the other lords and ladies of Altair hadn't known that she and her friends were responsible for the raids. Some stared at her with open loathing. Mikayla hadn't realized that the nobles represented the same towns and villages the girls had raided during the war. At the time, she had thought her actions were justified. The Pyxians were suffering and the girls had only destroyed forges, not the villages themselves. But now she understood that the NPCs who hadn't chosen to emigrate to Pyxis, the ones who had stayed in their ruined towns were still trying to repair the damage the girls had done. *No matter what we do, NPCs end up paying for it.*

"I thought you said what had happened in the war was over," Mikayla said. She felt the mistrust in their eyes as the Altairi stared at her.

"Otherwise you would have to answer for that shit you pulled on The Floating Eye," Brit said. "If we're still criminals, then what are you?"

"A king. One who has little patience for these insults. Did you come to participate in this summit or simply to bandy your baseless accusations about?"

"Baseless?" Now Suzanne was standing, nearly shouting at the king. "You started a phony war, destroyed half of Pyxis, and broke your own terms of peace. When are you going to really answer for that, Ramses? We fought and killed the Lamia for you, and instead of rewarding us you threw us in prison, remember? You want to know why we came back to Altair? We're still trying to get back to our home! We're not trying to steal your land, we're trying to leave it!"

What's she doing? Mikayla wondered. *Ramses doesn't need to know any of that.* "Shut up!" she hissed to Suzanne. They were letting Ramses goad them, revealing way too much.

A satisfied smile crept across the king's face. "It will be difficult for you to enter the Oracle Chamber without the key."

From within the folds of his robe, the king produced a key and set it on the table. It was golden, with a vein of green gemstone—Energite—running along its teeth. Mikayla noticed Suzanne lean forward, as if she was going to grab for the key. If Suzanne went for it, Mikayla wasn't about to stop her. If that key really did open the Oracle Chamber, and if Suzanne was right, that was all they needed to get home.

"Enough of this, Ramses," Rigel said. "None

of us came here to be insulted by your insinu-ations. We still have that cache of Energite to divvy up."

Burgrave cleared his throat. "The representa-tive from Pyxis speaks truly. We still have not heard from all the representatives. Might we return to the matter at hand?"

Xenos leaned forward and whispered some-thing into Ramses's ear. Mikayla thought she saw a flicker of disdain on Burgrave's face as the hooded NPC spoke. But it passed so quickly, Burgrave adopting his usual stoic expression, that she wasn't sure if she was imagining things.

Whatever Xenos had said seemed to please Ramses. He stowed the key back in his pocket. To Burgrave he said, "You are right, my coun-selors. Let us return to the Energite. I will keep my words pertinent to that subject and ask that all of you do the same. Lady Mikayla, you were saying?"

I was saying you're an arrogant asshole who's

responsible for everything wrong in Io, Mikayla thought. But the way the other NPCs were looking at her and her friends told her that she wasn't going to get anywhere with this crowd by saying that. Those that weren't under Ramses's thumb had been won to his side once he blamed the girls for the Pyxian raids.

Mikayla ignored them, returning Ramses's stare. She tried to keep her voice steady as she said, "I've already said everything there is to say. Zenith City needs Energite. The Citizens need more protection than we can offer."

She sat down as Ramses called on another Altairi noble, a Paladin with auburn hair. She was one of the few NPCs who was armed. From the way she glared at Ramses, Mikayla guessed this Paladin wasn't the king's biggest fan.

"My people are all refugees," she said. "We have come together for our own protection, not out of any sense of patriotism. I ask you all to do the same. Consider what your petty squabbles have done."

"Our so-called squabbles are for the right to rule!" Talleyrand exclaimed, banging a meaty hand on the table.

The Paladin scowled at him. "The wards have failed around our homes. The Citizens are all at risk. No one rules the dead, you toad. We must reunify if we are to have any hope at surviving."

The table broke out into muttering. So far none of the NPCs had suggested reunification for Altair. Ramses smiled even wider. Mikayla knew he was picturing himself as king of all Altair again.

"You speak with great conviction, Lady Mara," he said.

The name hit Mikayla like a thunderbolt. She glanced over at Suzanne—she was wide-eyed with shock. Brit looked like she was about to choke. Mikayla knew that Mara was going to be at the summit, but as she stared at the Paladin she felt a wave of guilt wash over her.

On Mara's armor were the same blue rings

which had been on the flags of her keep. From the way she was speaking, the Paladin must not have known what had happened to her people. *Should we tell her?* Mikayla wondered. How do you tell someone, even an NPC, that all of their subjects were dead?

She debated with herself through another hour of speeches. Then Ramses halted the summit for the day, saying they would resume the sessions the morning after next, to give everyone time to speak outside of the chamber. The NPCs filed out of the room, Mara going with them. Mikayla rose to follow her, but Brit grabbed her arm.

"What are you doing?" Brit whispered.

"We have to tell her," Mikayla hissed back.

"What are you going to say? 'Hey, my name's Mikayla. Nice to meet you. All your friends are dead'?"

"I don't know," Mikayla said, pulling her arm free. By then Mara was gone, as were the other

NPCs, leaving the girls alone in the conference room.

"You agree with me, right, Suzanne?"

Suzanne bit her lip. "We should tell her," she said. "I just don't know how we would."

Mikayla wondered the same thing as they went to find Mara. The other NPCs had gone to one of the banquet halls to have a meal. Mikayla ducked her head in, but there was no sign of the Paladin. Rigel waved to Mikayla, and she waved back, but she didn't go over to the NPC. She could see NPCs seating themselves by ideology. Most of the delegates were at a table with Talleyrand, loudly discussing their claims to the Energite. None of the Altairi would sit by the Pyxians.

"She wasn't in there," Mikayla said, exiting the banquet hall. They searched the gloomy grounds of Fenhold but didn't find the NPC there either. And the last thing Mikayla wanted to do was wander around Ramses's castle. With no other options, the girls climbed the tower back to their room. Rigel's guards snapped to attention as the girls reached their floor.

"We'll tell her tomorrow," Suzanne said, once they were inside. She didn't say it with much conviction.

Mikayla didn't answer her. Brit was already unequipping her gear and getting into bed. Looking out the window, Mikayla saw a beam of sunlight pierce through the canopy of the Fens. The wind blew, shifting the branches of the trees, snuffing the sunbeam out.

Chapter 8

"Listen," Brit said, jabbing her finger into the flab of Talleyrand's gut. "I don't give a shit whether or not you agree with what we're saying. If you don't quit following us around, you're going to be eating through a straw."

She didn't know if the NPC understood exactly what she was suggesting, but he understood the undercurrent of a threat well enough. Gulping, he tottered off as quickly as his stubby legs would carry him.

"Finally," Suzanne muttered.

Talleyrand had been following the girls around all day as they tried to speak with the various nobles. Suzanne, Mikayla, and Brit were trying to convince the Altairi that Ramses should answer for his war crimes and for getting Altair into a war in the first place.

Talleyrand had taken it upon himself to serve as devil's advocate, arguing against their proposals whenever they engaged an NPC. Brit didn't doubt that Ramses had put the fat NPC up to the task. Just because Talleyrand was a stooge for the king didn't mean he was precluded from eloquence.

Hopefully, now that he was gone, the girls would be able to make some headway. Talking to the NPCs was unsurprisingly Mikayla's idea. She was always coming up with crap like this. There was this one time when they were kids, like seven or eight, back when they would have playdates at Brit's house and the creek behind it. While splashing through the mud they found a raccoon that was pretty much roadkill. Someone had run it over, but the little critter managed to pull itself out of the road and down to the creek with the last of its strength.

Brit was all for dissection. At least she said she was. She would have never admitted how scared the sight of the animal's blood made her. But Mikayla was insistent that they bury the raccoon and hold a little raccoon funeral service. It wasn't like the raccoon cared one way or another, and no other raccoons came to attend the service. But afterwards, kneeling beside the refilled grave, Brit couldn't deny that she felt better about the whole thing. Their grave marker still stood, rain water having washed the faint etchings they made on a makeshift tombstone.

Mikayla suggested they split up to cover more ground during the recess, heading off on her own while Brit and Suzanne stuck together. Personally, Brit wanted to flex some muscle and force the NPCs to understand their point of view, but Mikayla had said that made them no better than Ramses.

Well, Brit didn't care all that much if they were better than Ramses. All she wanted was to leave Fenhold as soon as possible. The whole place gave her the creeps. And it wasn't just the gloomy atmosphere, though that certainly wasn't helping.

Earlier that day she spotted Samara and Desmond in the castle. Brit's stomach lurched when they passed by, blank expressions on their faces. Brit had fought with the Sniper and Defender against the Lamia. But when Brit and her friends were arrested, Desmond and Samara disappeared. There was no sign of them at all until they appeared on The Floating Eye, fighting for Ramses. Just as they hadn't seemed to recognize her during The Duels, they didn't seem to recognize Brit now.

It didn't make any sense. Brit nudged Suzanne and pointed the pair out. Desmond in particular was hard to miss. His bulky Defender's frame made him stick out in a crowd.

"What are they doing here?" Suzanne whispered.

"I guess they're still working for Ramses," Brit replied. That much was obvious. But where they were headed—back into the castle, away from all the other NPCs—well, that was more interesting.

There was no need for them to discuss the matter. Brit and Suzanne began to follow them.

The Defender and the Sniper wove their way through the network of Fenhold's hallways, back to the room where everyone assembled when they all arrived. Desmond held the door for Samara as she slipped aside and pulled it shut behind them. Brit waited for a moment before grabbing the handle.

"Wait," Suzanne said. "Someone's coming."

Brit could hear the footsteps too. Casually, she flipped open her inventory and reached for a halberd. If they needed to, they could fight their way out of here. *But how would you tell Mikayla?* She didn't have an answer for that.

Luckily, it wasn't going to be a fight. Mara rounded the corner, deep in conversation with a Citizen in gilded robes. Brit remembered the Citizen saying he was from the northwest of the kingdom, back by where the girls had killed the Lamia. Brit thought those villages had been deserted, but apparently there were NPCs in them now.

"Hail conquerors!" the Paladin joked, waving to them. The Citizen beside her blanched at the sight of the girls. Brit grinned. At least there was an NPC who didn't think they were bloodthirsty murderers. But then her mind went to thoughts of Mara's people and the grin fell off her face.

"What's up?" she asked.

"We were just discussing our mutual interests," Mara said. "Elijah has agreed that reunification is in our best interest."

"You can't seriously want to join back up with Ramses," Suzanne said.

Mara shook her head. "Certainly not. As I

said, my aim is to join back up with all of Altair. Together we can weather these monsters."

"Even with Ramses at the head of things?" Brit asked.

"Who said anything about Ramses as ruler?" Mara replied.

"Therein lies your problem," Elijah squeaked. "No one but Ramses could unite us. I would rather die than serve the mad king again!"

Mara chuckled. "Your confidence is always refreshing." Turning to Brit and Suzanne she said, "We were just leaving this dismal castle for some fresh air. Please, join us."

Brit and Suzanne exchanged a look. If they left their post by the door then they'd miss Desmond and Samara when they came back out. The longer they hung out with Mara, the more likely they were to let something about the inn drop. The Paladin was one of their only allies at the summit. If they let her know what had happened there was no way she would stick around once she heard. Then the girls would only have Rigel to count on.

Brit felt especially uncomfortable around the Paladin, considering the dream she'd had the previous night.

Once more, she was in the blazing courtyard of Mara's fort, and once more Rogues were pouring over the walls, slaughtering at will.

A knife flew from a Rogue's hand. Brit caught the blade on the shaft of her halberd. The Rogue pulled out another knife, but before he could throw it Brit was upon him. With a two-handed swing she struck him down. A foot on his chest made sure he wouldn't get back up.

"Nice try," she said. She raised her halberd high.

But then the Rogue changed. His black cloak melted away, his features reassembling themselves into Joaquin's. Brit tried to check her swing, but some force drove her halberd down harder. The blow split Joaquin's skull into pixels.

Brit staggered off Joaquin's pixelating body. Before she could truly register what had happened, she saw another Rogue. The second Rogue didn't even try to fight. She turned and fled for the gate. As fast as she was, Brit was faster, overtaking the Rogue easily. She grabbed the Rogue by the shoulders and threw her into the blazing walls of Mara's fort.

It was like someone else was controlling Brit's body. And then suddenly Brit was watching herself, disembodied and floating above the carnage. Brit watched as her own body stalked toward the downed Rogue, dragging her halberd behind her. She looked like some kind of monster. The Rogue struggled up to her feet, and her hood fell away.

It was Gwynedd.

"Please," Gwynedd said, "you don't have to this."

Brit's body made no response. A massive hand grabbed Gwynedd around the throat and lifted her into the air. Gwynedd kicked and struggled but nothing could make the iron fingers relent.

Brit was helpless to do anything. She tried to will herself back in control of her body but remained removed. She tried to shout, but she had no voice. And so she watched as her body choked the life out Gwynedd. She watched as Gwynedd was thrown aside, limp and pixelating.

That was when Brit woke up. She sat in her bed flexing her hand over and over again, making sure that she was still in control. Tactile memories lingered from the dream like bruises. It felt like she had just been gripping her halberd, like her hands had just been around Gwynedd's neck.

Brit flexed her hand again. She was so wrapped up in her memory that she was barely following the conversation. Suzanne, Mara, and Elijah were still debating the merits of reunification. But they could have been speaking Russian, for all their words meant to Brit. Brit told herself, *It was just a dream. It wasn't you.* But even if it wasn't her fault, that didn't change what had happened. That didn't change how guilty she felt whenever she looked at Mara.

"So who would you pick to lead?" Suzanne asked.

Mara thought before answering. "It should not just be my choice. It would have to be the representative from one of the larger cities. Otherwise, how could they gain popular support? We would need a proven warrior, but one who wasn't given to conquering like Ramses. The last thing Altair needs is another war. No, what we need is a peaceful and just ruler. But unless they can command the respect of the mighty, their peace will be for nothing."

To Brit it sounded like Mara was suggesting

they enthrone Mikayla. But she didn't bring that up.

Mara pointed to the interlocking blue circles emblazoned on her armor. "That is the reasoning behind my sigil. The three rings stand for peace, justice, and strength. Yet without one, the other two are meaningless. We cannot settle for two of these principles and allow the third to wither."

They left through a side door in Fenhold, crossing into the shadowy grounds. The ebony walls melted into the twilight, making Brit feel claustrophobic. Even within the castle grounds, Brit could hear the screeching and howling of monsters in the swamp. As little as she liked Fenhold, she wasn't excited to tromp back through the swamp.

She saw Suzanne shudder. Brit understood the response. "Ramses sure loves this gloomy shit," Brit said.

Elijah looked scandalized at her insulting the king, but didn't argue the point. Brit wondered if he was scared of her. She remembered how afraid Gwynedd had looked in her dream.

"What do you think we should do with the Energite?" Mara was asking. It took Brit a second to realize the Paladin was talking to her.

"Me?" she managed to sputter out.

"Yes, you. You've traveled extensively in both Altair and Pyxis. Your three views on the matter are perhaps the best informed."

Brit thought for a moment. "I have no idea," she said, forcing a laugh. "I never really thought about it."

"Then why did you come to this summit in the first place?" There was a note of annoyance in the Paladin's voice, but she seemed genuinely curious as well.

"Ramses has some shit to answer for," Brit said. She felt like she was repeating herself. But Mara nodded like she understood.

"And after you've gotten your vengeance?" she asked.

Suzanne cut in. "Then we'll leave, assuming we can. We'll go home."

"Not to Pyxis," Brit added hastily, seeing the confusion on Mara's face. "We're, uh, from a place called Baltimore. It's very far away from here."

Mara frowned. "I've never heard of this Baltimore," she said.

Elijah muttered something. To Brit, it sounded like "meddling foreigners." She glared down at the Citizen, who retreated a tactful step away.

"It's a pity," Mara said. "I would appreciate having three allies in the rebuilding process. But if you must go, then go you must."

They had wandered over to a cluster of stone benches by Fenhold's western wall. Mara took a seat, leaning against the wall.

"What I want is for my people not to be afraid. That is silly, isn't it? I can't stop everything from hurting them. But there has been so much pain and confusion lately and I want to save them from that."

Brit didn't know what to say. She pictured Gwynedd, the Citizen who went with her to patrol the fortified inn. She could still hear the thunk and gurgle as the arrow pierced Gwynedd's throat.

"I'm sure your people are at peace," Suzanne said. Brit tried to catch her, but Suzanne looked away, staring at the wall.

Mara smiled. "I am sure you are right. But enough of our talk! As pleasant as it has been, we each have our duties, do we not? There are many more I need to speak with before we convene tomorrow."

She left them at the benches, promising she would see them the next day. Once she was gone, Elijah turned to the girls, sneering.

"Don't think the rest of us have forgotten what you did," he said. "You might be here on behalf of Zenith City, but the Capital must be

desperate if they sent you three. You're all trai-
tors to Altair."

Is he serious? "Dude," Brit said. "We aren't
even Altairi."

"You betrayed the king's trust!" Elijah
squeaked. "You raided our villages for the Pyxians! How can you look me or any decent Altairi
in the face after all you've done?"

"That's the thing," Brit said. "We still haven't
met a decent Altairi."

Quivering with rage, Elijah stalked off, leaving
Brit and Suzanne alone.

It had been a while since the two of them
spent any time together. Brit hadn't failed to
notice how quiet Suzanne had been lately. She
was all wrapped up in herself, which wasn't
unusual for Suze, but lately she had been even
more standoffish than usual. Something had to
be eating her. Well, Brit never avoided the direct
route if it was available.

"How're you doing?" Brit asked.

Suzanne shrugged.

"Do you miss Leo?"

Suze flipped her off. That was good. At least she was capable of feeling something.

"Missing those hot cyber smooches?" Brit asked.

"Hey, screw you," Suzanne said, laughing. But that was only with her mouth. Her eyes remained clouded.

Brit leaned forward, dropping her voice so eavesdroppers couldn't hear. "Listen, Suze, do me a favor and forget about the inn, okay?"

"Sure," Suzanne said.

"No, listen—I'm being serious. You've got to focus on what's happening now, okay? We can't make it out of here without you. You're the only one who has any fucking idea what's going on."

Suzanne frowned, but didn't argue the point. "Come on," she said. "We've got to go talk to more NPCs."

Brit wasn't looking forward to hearing more

NPCs call her a traitor. Suzanne looked as excited as Brit felt.

"Or," Brit said, "hear me out. We could not do that and just tell Mikayla we did. It's not like we're changing any minds anyway."

Suzanne laughed, and this time it sounded like she really meant it. "Yeah, right. Like you could lie to Mikayla."

"And what's that supposed to mean?"

"You know exactly what I mean. Tell me one secret you've ever kept from her."

"Um," Brit said.

She could think of a few things she hadn't told Mikayla. Most notably, she hadn't told Mikayla about her dreams yet. But she was also keeping that secret from Suzanne. *Suze doesn't need anything else to worry about,* Brit told herself. And anything else she was keeping away from Mikayla—well, it didn't make sense to tell Suzanne either. Forcing a laugh, Brit said,

"You're right. I guess we're gonna have to talk to more NPCs."

Chapter 9

Mikayla was sitting on top of Fenhold's southern wall. She had been speaking with the representative from Riversforge, the first village the Pyxians sabotaged during the war. Every time Mikayla thought she was close to getting through to the NPC, he doubled-down on the fact that the girls had helped with the sabotage. Accordingly, he swore he couldn't trust her.

It was beyond frustrating. She could see the gears turning in his head, see him about to change his mind, but then like clockwork he'd blurt out something about sabotage. After the fifth time,

Mikayla was more than willing to write him off as a lost cause.

That was the fifteenth NPC Mikayla talked to that day. So far he'd been the most receptive to what she was saying. She wondered if Brit and Suzanne were having any more luck. Then she thought of Brit's diplomatic prowess and had to laugh.

The wall looked over the Fens south of Ramses's castle. Mikayla had to admit, as much as she hated traveling through the Fens, from this angle they weren't half bad. She had never been a kid who went to nature preserves. Her parents pushed studying and extracurriculars over things like vacation. Summer break was spent in accelerator programs, learning math so she could catch up with the "advanced students."

Sometimes the world of Io staggered her with its alien beauty. Take the Fens as an example. Suburban Baltimore—where Mikayla was from—was many things, but it was not a wild swamp. She came from a land of sidewalks and strip malls, nothing like the teeming Fens.

She let herself become enchanted by the mist rising off the Fens, its tendrils winding around the creepers and vines. With her heightened vision, she could see creatures in the mist, the grey icons marking them twirling lazily over their heads. In a tree there was a whole cluster of ratlings, half-rat, half-human hybrids. Up close, Mikayla thought they were gross with their hairy snouts, slavering jaws, and bloodshot eyes. But from a distance they were kind of cute, more furry than furious.

Is it a family? Two of the ratlings were much larger than the others. They were all in a nest, the small ones leaning on the big ones. Sometimes she saw monsters fighting each other in the wilderness, but these monsters seemed content to just lie there. It was the most peaceful Mikayla had ever seen a ratling, and that peace infected her, calming the frustrations of the day.

"Lady Mikayla."

Mikayla jumped. She hadn't heard any footsteps approaching. But there was Burgrave, his earrings swishing as he walked along the wall toward her.

"Burgrave." She stood up and tried to seem unfazed, but she was willing to bet Burgrave saw through that right away. This was the first time she had been alone with Burgrave since their duel on The Floating Eye. She reached for a sword before remembering that she had put them away so she wouldn't scare the NPCs. Of course, that hadn't really mattered.

Burgrave stopped a few feet away from her and bowed solemnly. The fastidious little NPC always looked so serious, which was why Mikayla almost laughed when he asked, "How are you enjoying the summit so far?"

What does he think this is? But she didn't want to get into an argument with another NPC. So she said, "The castle is very comfortable."

Apparently, that was enough to satisfy Burgrave, as he didn't ask anything else immediately. He turned and regarded the ratlings in the tree.

"Do you know if that's a family?" she asked.

"A what?"

"A family. Those ratlings in the tree. You know, mama ratling, papa ratling, a few baby ratlings?"

"I do not know," he replied.

"Where I come from—where we come from—animals have families just like we do. Where else would the babies come from?"

Burgrave stared at her. "I had not thought of that," he admitted. "I have only ever been concerned with monsters inasmuch as they present a threat to the Citizens."

"Sometimes people raise whole families of animals, you know, like pets."

"Pets." Burgrave tried the word out. Suddenly, Mikayla felt beyond foolish. What was she doing discussing pets with Burgrave? There were other

NPCs she could try convincing. Burgrave was such a Ramses fanboy that Mikayla wondered how he could maintain a civil tone with her.

She rose to go, but he said, "Please wait." Something in his tone made her stop and listen for what he had to say.

"Why are you trying to convince the other delegates to charge Ramses with crimes?"

Mikayla laughed. "Because he's guilty."

"Whether or not that's true—"

"It is," Mikayla said, doing her best to channel Brit's obstinance.

"Whether or not that's true, wouldn't it be better to spend your time trying to secure a claim for the Citizens in the suburbs? That was who you came to represent, correct? Even if you succeed with your current course, who will get Energite for those Citizens?"

Mikayla didn't have an answer for him.

"You must not let your hatred of Ramses blind you."

"If you're so concerned about the Citizens in the suburbs then why did you leave them there without any protection? What are you doing all the way down here in a swamp?"

"My place is by the king," Burgrave said. But Mikayla had heard that tune before.

"That's bullshit," she said. "You're only here because you want to be here. You could do so much good for your people, but you'd rather just do what the king says. That way, you don't have to make any decisions for yourself."

He took a step back and blinked. Mikayla was surprised by her own vehemence; she wasn't going to stand here and get lectured by one of Ramses's henchmen. Burgrave looked away from her, back at the ratlings in their nest. She wondered if she had offended the NPC. She wondered if Burgrave could even be offended. He always maintained the same placid demeanor, but there had to be something more going on underneath the facade.

"This is not the first time you have said such things to me," Burgrave spoke softly.

Mikayla didn't know what to say. Far above them, the scattering of light that beached the canopy changed, turning golden with the setting sun. Off in the Fens, the primarily nocturnal monsters began to wake up. Mikayla could hear the far-off cry of screechers flying nearer.

"I could say, 'You are new to our land. I have lived here my whole life. You do not understand.'" Burgrave shook his head. "That would be a lie. You see as much as I do, perhaps even more. I wonder if you have seen the cycle yet."

"The cycle?"

"Each day we rise. We fight monsters. We mine what resources we need from the land and forge them into what items we require. The weak become strong, the strong become stronger. Each day, more monsters appear, more items are forged, more experience gained. We expend our energy and recoup it. The cycle persists."

Burgrave paused as a screecher flapped by, howling into the dusk. As it neared the tower of Fenhold, one of the Altairi soldiers shot it out of the sky with an arrow. The screecher was pixels before its body hit the ground.

He was describing the game's daily reset. Mikayla knew that each night the monsters respawned to replenish their numbers. It made sense that the NPCs had observed the phenomenon.

"There is that cycle," Burgrave continued, "and there is another. This one runs deeper. We come into the world, we grow. We fight or do not fight and then we die. Our bodies become nothing, the same nothing that everything else is made of. From nothing we come and to the nothingness we return."

Ashes to ashes, Mikayla thought, *dust to dust.*

"What does this have to do with Ramses?" she asked.

"Our lives are so short," Burgrave said. "In

the face of the world, they are nothing. I aim to make the lives of as many as palatable for the short time they are here. By serving Ramses, I have done this."

"You can't seriously still believe that," Mikayla said. "If it wasn't for Ramses, then there would have never been a war."

"There is always conflict. That is part of the cycle as well."

"Then your cycle is bullshit! Just because people are going to fight doesn't mean you have to stand by and let them! Or worse, help spread the fight."

"That is where we disagree. The conflict is inevitable as long as Ramses remains in power. To remove him from power would cause even more conflict. Look at the state of Altair now and tell me that Ramses removed from Zenith City has brought peace."

"It's not about right now," she said. "It's about tomorrow. Not this run of the cycle but the next one. In the future, when there no longer is a Ramses or a Burgrave or a Mikayla, what we did today will still matter. So you can't just say there will always be conflict. You can't know! All you can do is help make tomorrow better!"

Mikayla heard clapping, then footsteps. Brit and Suzanne climbed up onto the battlement and walked toward her.

"Great speech," Brit said sarcastically.

Damn it, Brit! Mikayla thought. *I was getting through to him!*

Burgrave bowed to her. "As always, you have given me much to think about." He excused himself and hurried away.

"You scared him off!" Mikayla said.

Brit laughed. "I don't think that dude is scared of anyone."

"Come on, Brit! You know what I mean. He was listening to me."

"So what?" Brit said.

Mikayla hated it when Brit got like this. Why couldn't she just take things seriously, for once?

"So what?"

"Uh, guys," Suzanne said. "You're shouting. We could hear you and Burgrave all the way across the courtyard. Let's not shout everything to the entire castle, okay?"

Brit shrugged, unfazed. Mikayla glared at her. She saw Suzanne glancing anxiously between the two of them, getting that worried look she had whenever an argument started.

Mikayla sighed. "I'm sorry I snapped at you, Brit. But all the NPCs I talked to have been such assholes and Burgrave was actually listening to me!"

"I accept your apology," Brit replied with mock solemnity.

Mikayla was about to flare up at her again but Brit waved her hands in front of her. "Joking! I'm joking! I'm sorry I screwed that up."

Brit sat down, her armor clattering against the

stone parapet. "We didn't have any luck either. That tool Talleyrand followed us around for a bit until I scared him off."

Mikayla slid down so she was sitting at Brit's level. "NPCs," she muttered, shaking her head. "Aren't they supposed to listen to us?

"I'll have to fix the algorithm so they do," Suzanne offered.

She was pacing back and forth.

"Where do you have to be?" Brit asked Suzanne, stating the question on Mikayla's mind.

"Nowhere," Suzanne said. "I just wanted to see if Samara and Desmond ever came back out."

"What's she talking about?" Mikayla asked.

Brit explained that they'd seen Desmond and Samara. Mikayla wasn't surprised to hear that the two of them were lurking around the castle. Earlier they must have blended in with the other advanced class NPCs in Ramses's retinue.

"Let's swing by there on our way back to the

room," Mikayla suggested. Suzanne was clearly dying to check up on them anyway.

As they entered the hall, the door creaked open and Ramses stepped out, accompanied by Xenos, Desmond, Samara, and other guards Mikayla didn't recognize. He saw them coming in and stopped long enough to ask, "Don't you have some innocents to murder?" before continuing on his way.

"You didn't say Ramses was in there with them," Mikayla said.

"I didn't know!" Suzanne said. She sounded giddy.

"What's got you so happy?" Mikayla asked. Mikayla didn't like the look in Suzanne's eyes. There was a look of recklessness that Mikayla would've expected from Brit.

"If he was in there, that means those are his chambers," Suzanne whispered excitedly. "I can grab the key from him tonight! Then tomorrow we can go home!"

Mikayla wasn't so sure. "Don't you think Ramses might just be messing with us? I mean really, what are the chances that the key even works?"

"We could still shake him down," Brit suggested. "Get him when he's not surrounded by his guards."

Mikayla shook her head. "We shouldn't pick a fight on Ramses's home turf when we're at such a disadvantage. The Altairi hate us enough already. Besides, Ramses always has Xenos with him, and I don't think we can handle that guy. Something about him just feels . . . off."

There was no arguing with that.

"So we came all this way for nothing?" Brit sounded disappointed. Mikayla wished she had something better to tell her.

"We'll get a chance," Mikayla said. "We just have to wait for the right time to make our move. Right, Suzanne?"

Suzanne didn't answer. She was staring out the

window, in her own little world. Mikayla sighed. If they weren't careful, none of them were going to be leaving the Fenlands.

Chapter 10

Suzanne pulled on her cloak and took a grappling hook out of her inventory. She stood dead still, listening to Brit snoring. Brit shouldn't be snoring. Their player characters weren't supposed to move while the girls were asleep. But it was just one more thing on Suzanne's to-do list for when they got out.

When she was sure Brit wasn't awake, Suzanne walked over to the window. She knew the room below theirs was empty. It was a short climb down and then she'd be free to explore the castle without waking Brit and Mikayla, and without alerting the guard Rigel had stuck outside their door. She had hesitated, balking at the window.

Come on, she told herself. *Stop being such a baby and go get that key.*

Ramses had the key. He said it would open the Oracle Chamber, and had waved it in her face. She wanted the key to get back to the real world, obviously, but swiping it from Ramses only sweetened the deal. It was clear to Suzanne that the girls weren't going to get any help from Ramses. This whole summit struck her as a chance for the king to flex his power on his home turf. And the way the other Altairi swallowed every bit of bullshit he fed them . . . none of that would matter if Suzanne could get the key. All of it: Ramses, his pet nobles, and even the Fenlands were just more code to rewrite once she was out of the game.

But before Suzanne could fix them, she would have to get that key. And still she hesitated. She could almost hear Mikayla asking, "What if it doesn't work?" *If it doesn't work then we're no better off. Worst case scenario, I climb back in the window and go to sleep.* "And what about his guards?" Mikayla would ask. "You know he won't be easy to get to." But Suzanne knew that the guards wouldn't stop her if they couldn't see her. And she knew how to move around Io unseen.

Maybe it was fine for Brit and Mikayla to keep playing the game. They had certainly done that in Zenith City, Suzanne realized, drilling the Citizens while she was working on opening the Oracle Chamber. If they wanted to play politics at the summit, that was fine, too. But Suzanne had to go after that key. It was their best chance of leaving the Fenlands with anything more than frustration.

Suzanne secured the grappling hook on the window sill and dropped the rope. It extended well beyond the window one floor below. She jerked the rope to test how it held; satisfied, she ducked through the window and began to lower herself down. Descending hand-over-hand, gripping the rope with her knees, Suzanne quickly found herself outside the lower floor's window. Suzanne paused, listening for a sign of NPCs in the room.

There was a sound from far below her; Suzanne looked down to see Burgrave stepping out of a postern door. She knew it was him by the way the moonlight gleamed off his bald head. Burgrave hustled across the cleared land surrounding the castle, vanishing into the tangle of the Fenlands. *Good,* Suzanne thought. *That's one less of them to worry about.*

She paused before entering the lower room. Hanging, suspended as she was outside the tower, the Fenlands were breathtaking. On the ground, they were a mess of swamp and vine; viewed from above, free from having to actually go through them, the Fenlands had a mystical beauty of their own. What moonlight made it through the canopy fell like pearlescent snow across the map. Mist rose off the swamp, wrapping the world in a prehistoric glamour. Even the monsters calling to each other took on another aspect when viewed from above. In the scattered moonlight, they were but shadows calling out to each other, their cries a chorus of hoots and howls.

This was what Suzanne pictured when building the Fens line by line on a screen. She took it as a good omen as she slipped through the window.

Landing noiselessly, she waited by the window for her eyes to readjust to the darkness within the castle. Once she could see, she padded silently toward the door. She listened until she was sure she heard no footsteps, eased the door open, and then slipped out into the stairs.

She fired off a Shadow Walk immediately. As long as she stayed quiet and in the shadows, she would be virtually invisible to NPCs for the duration of the special move. In Pyxis, Energite had been easy enough to find, but it was still scarce in Altair. Suzanne had been preserving her Energite levels while she was in Altair, but she needed to use them now.

Suzanne heard the guards Rigel had set by her door pacing on the landing above. That was good. If they had noticed she was gone, they would have come looking for her. Still, she descended the tower stairs quickly; Shadow Walk would cover her, but it wouldn't do to get cornered on the narrow stairwell.

At the base of the tower she paused again, but there was no need. The hall connecting the tower to the rest of the castle was as empty as the stairs had been. At night, the shadows of Fenhold were even deeper than during the day. As glad as Suzanne was to have cover, she was still unnerved by the shadows. *It's like one of those black-and-white horror movies,* she thought. Nosferatu could be coming around the corner.

She almost pulled one of the empty sconces on the wall to see if it opened a secret passage.

She followed the hallways toward the center of Fenhold, trying to find her way back to the room where she'd seen Ramses earlier. If those were his quarters, that's where the key would be. Ramses probably slept with it. Well, if Suzanne had to take him out to get what she wanted, then that was one less obnoxious king the girls had to deal with. She could picture Brit complaining that she didn't get a shot at Ramses. Suzanne stifled a laugh and moved on.

It was tricky navigating Fenhold in the dark. Suzanne peered around every corner, making sure she stayed out of any guard's line of sight. After a few wrong turns, she found her way to the right hall. The massive doors wouldn't budge when she pulled on them. That was hardly a surprise. Suzanne's character was better at picking locks than yanking doors open.

Just when she was about to start on picking

the lock, footsteps echoed down the hall. Suzanne pressed herself flat against the wall, melting into the shadows. The guards that walked past her never so much as looked in her direction. They were right in front of her when they walked into a sliver of torchlight, revealing them to be Desmond and Samara. Samara opened the door and slipped inside. The Defender followed, Suzanne ducking in right before the doors shut after him.

Once inside, Desmond and Samara made for the dais at the center of the chamber. Suzanne followed them at a distance, hugging the wall where the shadows were deepest. The Sniper leapt nimbly onto the dais. She scanned the room, looking for intruders. Suzanne held her breath, but she needn't have bothered; she was completely hidden by her Shadow Walk. Suzanne watched Samara drop to her hands and knees, searching around the dais for something. She heard a click as the Sniper flipped open a trap door. *Maybe I should have tried the sconce,*

Suzanne thought. Samara and Desmond stepped down into the trap door. It swung shut behind them, the sound of its closing echoing off the walls.

Was Ramses down there? Even if he wasn't, Suzanne knew she was going to follow the NPCs down. The clandestine way Samara had looked around the chamber suggested that there was something down there Ramses didn't want the other NPCs to know about. Suzanne counted to ten, waiting for the NPCs to descend far enough. Then she climbed up onto the dais and felt around for the grooves of the door. She found a seam in the stone but couldn't find a latch to pull the door open with. It looked like she would have to make her own.

She grabbed a dagger off her belt and slid the blade into the groove. Leaning on the dagger, she jimmied the trap door up. When it was high enough to slip a finger through, she grabbed the door and threw it back. It slammed against the stone with a loud bang. But if any NPCs above or below heard, none came to investigate the noise. Suzanne found the first step down into the trap door and began the descent down.

The stairs she followed were as tall as the tower steps it seemed. Suzanne went slowly; the last thing she wanted was to overtake Desmond and Samara. At the bottom of the stairs was another hallway. But unlike the hallways above, this one had a rounded ceiling, more of a tunnel than a hall. The walls were rough, hewn instead of built. Pale light filled the tunnel, nauseous green in hue. The air was so cold that Suzanne shivered. Never before had she felt temperature like this in Io. It was like she had stepped into a walk-in freezer. Exhaling through her mouth, she half-expected to see her breath condensing from the cold.

There was orange light at the end of the hall, flickering against the walls up ahead. Suzanne could make out the soft murmur of voices. She crept forward, withdrawing her daggers. In the tunnel there was absolutely nowhere to hide. If it came to a fight, she had to be ready.

The murmuring voices grew more distinct as Suzanne approached the end of the tunnel. " . . . the key. Suzanne must not discover the true key."

Suzanne froze when she heard her name. She didn't recognize the voice; its cold monotone was alien and discomfiting. It sounded nothing like Burgrave, who strove to speak without emotion, yet inevitably some slipped through. No, this voice was like a computer reading words, pronouncing them without thinking. It wasn't because of the coldness of the tunnel that Suzanne shivered.

"Suzanne must not discover," a second voice mumbled. That was Ramses's voice! So she had found the king down in the tunnels. But the quality of Ramses's voice also disturbed her. Free of the sneering malice he usually possessed,

Ramses sounded like a different NPC, like he was talking in his sleep.

Curiosity overcame her unease and Suzanne forced herself to the end of the tunnel. The room she stepped into was filled with the same pale light as the tunnel. It was completely empty, except for two chairs with a torch set in a brazier between them. In one of them Ramses slouched, arms dangling at his sides and his eyes shut. His mouth hung open in an imbecilic expression.

Xenos sat in the other chair. Even here, down in the tunnels, his hood was pulled low over his face. The chairs faced each other. The NPCs appeared to be so focused on each other that they didn't notice Suzanne crouched at the edge of the room.

"Get rid of the other two. They are distractions," Xenos pronounced. *So that was his voice!* Suzanne thought. Thinking back on all the times she had seen Xenos, Suzanne couldn't remember ever hearing him speak before. Hearing the words come out of his mouth did nothing to quell the uneasy feeling Xenos's voice provoked in her.

"Get rid of the other two," Ramses repeated.

They had to be talking about Brit and Mikayla! But why was Xenos telling Ramses to get rid of them and not her? Part of her screamed to turn back and get away while she still could. She had no idea where Desmond and Samara had gotten to. If it was just Ramses, Suzanne might have been able to take him even with the Defender and the Sniper . . . but Xenos was a different story. If she moved fast enough, she could get back to Brit and Mikayla before Ramses followed Xenos's advice and tried to get rid of them. Rigel could help. Her friends needed to know what was going on, and Suzanne was the only one who could tell them.

But she didn't move. She stayed there, crouched at the mouth of the tunnel, watching. Xenos leaned forward and placed his palm on the king's forehead. His palm began to glow, brighter and brighter, dwarfing the fire with its glare until Suzanne could no longer look directly at the NPCs. The light passed to Ramses's forehead, fading into the skin of the king. Ramses's eyes snapped open and he sat up straight in the chair. Ramses looked over the entire room, his eyes passing Suzanne without seeing her due to the last remnant of her Shadow Walk.

"Xenos," the king said. Suzanne noticed that the king did not look directly at the other NPC. *Ramses is afraid of him*, she realized.

"My king."

"Let us move above ground," the king said, his voice shaky. "I do not like being down here."

"Certainly. Gemini, clear the way."

Gemini? Suzanne whirled around; too late. A kick smashed into her face, slamming her head into the wall of the tunnel. Groggy, Suzanne fell to her knees. She saw Gemini standing in the pale light of the tunnel. *When did she get here?*

"You really thought you were hiding?" Gemini

asked. "Seriously? We can all see through that cute little Shadow Walk of yours."

Gemini kicked at her head again, but this time Suzanne was ready. She caught the Assassin's foot at the ankle and pulled. Gemini hopped forward to keep her balance. Suzanne jabbed at the Assassin's other foot, knocking it out from under her and dropping Gemini to the floor.

Bracing herself against the wall, Suzanne rose shakily to standing. She drew her daggers and backed into the room with Ramses and Xenos. "How dare you!" the king shouted. "You are not allowed to be down here! I'll throw you and your little friends in the dungeon, like I should have the second you showed your faces in the Fens!"

Suzanne ignored him. She kept her eyes on Xenos, but the hooded NPC merely sat in his chair. "What is the true key?" she asked him.

"You do not know, Miss Thurston?" he

replied. "That is good. I was afraid you might have figured it out."

Figured out what? But Gemini was getting up, her curved knives glittering in the wan tunnel light. Any questions Suzanne had would have to wait until the Assassin was down.

Gemini moved faster than Suzanne could have imagined, slashing at Suzanne's face and waist. Suzanne stepped backwards and lashed out with her own dagger, stabbing nothing but air. Too late she saw Gemini's knife arcing downwards, gashing her arm. Suzanne felt a chunk of her health bar fall away. It was just like her duel with Gemini on The Floating Eye. No matter what she did, the Assassin seemed to be a step ahead.

But it wasn't a duel. Suzanne didn't have to win or fight fair, she just had to get away. Gemini lunged at her again and Suzanne cart-wheeled out of the way. She grabbed a throwing knife from her belt and flung it at Ramses.

The king screamed as the blade planted itself in his stomach, tumbling backwards out of his chair. His foot lashed out and knocked over the brazier, scattering the embers of the fire. They extinguished as soon as they hit the floor.

"No!" Gemini shouted, running to Ramses's side. *Now's my chance*, Suzanne thought, grabbing a smoke bomb out of her inventory. She threw the bomb at the king and sprinted toward the tunnel. But when she reached the tunnel she stopped; the bomb had not exploded.

Turning back, she saw Xenos pointing at the smoke bomb. The bomb hovered inches off the ground, wrapped in the same bright light that had passed between Xenos and Ramses earlier. The light dissipated and the bomb fell to the ground, clattering on the stone, a dud. *How was Xenos doing all of this?*

Suzanne watched, transfixed, as the hooded NPC rose from his chair and walked to Ramses's side. Brushing past Gemini, Xenos grabbed

Suzanne's throwing knife and yanked it out. Then he pulled Ramses to his feet like the king weighed no more than a feather. The king looked fine; Suzanne couldn't see a wound from where the knife was embedded a moment earlier.

"Sleep," Xenos said, and Ramses shut his eyes.

Suzanne knew there was no way she could fight against these NPCs. She had to run. But when she turned back, the tunnel was no longer there. She was in a room with no exits, trapped with Gemini and Xenos.

She held her dagger in front of her, trying to ignore how her hand shook. The sickly green light that filled the room seemed to grow deeper. Xenos advanced toward her, his hand raised. Suzanne felt like she had to vomit. The room spun as she dropped again to her hands and knees.

"You have become something of a problem, Miss Thurston," Xenos said, neither anger nor displeasure apparent in his tone. "We simply cannot allow that to continue."

Right before she blacked out, Suzanne realized that was the second time Xenos had called her by her last name.

Chapter 11

"Where the fuck is she?" Brit was shouting, but Mikayla knew she was more worried than angry. She had woken up early that morning and Suzanne had been gone. That alone wasn't enough to worry Mikayla. She began to feel uncomfortable when Suzanne still wasn't back when Brit woke up a few hours later. It was only when Brit asked where Suzanne was that Mikayla found the grappling hook on the window sill and the rope hanging from it. Suzanne had gone out the window sometime last night, that much Mikayla knew for certain.

But where Suzanne went and where Suzanne was were two questions Mikayla couldn't answer.

Rigel's guards were no help at all. They hadn't seen anyone last night, but if Suzanne had climbed down the rope to the floor below, then they wouldn't have seen her going down the stairs anyway. She asked the captain if he had heard anything and he answered with noncommittal bullshit. Maybe he heard something but it could have been any number of things. Mikayla gave up; if Suzanne hadn't wanted the guards to see her, then she could have slipped past them easily enough.

Mikayla knew they couldn't just wait around the room all day hoping Suzanne came back. The second day of the summit was starting soon, and if they were late Ramses would seize the opportunity to attack them in front of the other nobles again. As Mikayla dressed, she made sure to strap on her swords. With Suzanne missing, she was on edge; her swords made her feel safer, even if she wasn't planning on using them.

Brit made an impressive sight, armor rattling as they climbed down the tower stairs. In the real world, Brit was just as determined, but she lacked the muscle to back it up. That wasn't a problem in Io. It was almost like Brit's character was who she really was.

Mikayla paused at the cross halls, searching for Suzanne's face among the NPCs bustling around the castle. But there was no sight of Suzanne's black, braided hair in all of Fenhold.

They did find Rigel and the rest of the Pyxians by the castle's entrance. They had barely seen the old Monk since the first day of the summit. To Mikayla's dismay, she saw that the Pyxians were dressed for travel.

"Suzanne's missing," Brit blurted out, before Rigel could greet them.

The Pyxian's face creased into a frown. "You

sure? This is a big castle. Could be she went for a walk."

Mikayla shook her head. "She climbed out the window last night. I've been up all morning and she hasn't come back." She explained to Rigel about the grappling hook and rope, and how his guard's hadn't heard anything. "Why go to all the trouble if she was just walking around?" she asked him.

"But where would she go that she wouldn't want the two of you knowing?"

"The key!" Brit shouted. Altairi nobles passing by turned to look. Mikayla glared at Brit, who sheepishly whispered, "That key that Ramses waved around yesterday! I bet Suze went to steal it. She probably thought you'd stop her if you knew."

"And you wouldn't have?" Mikayla asked. "You think it's smart to go creeping around Ramses's castle alone?"

"I didn't say that. But come on, you know

Suze. Ramses said that key would open the Oracle Chamber and that's all she's been trying to do for the past month."

That made sense. It would certainly explain why Suzanne had been so secretive about leaving. But if she had gone looking for Ramses and she hadn't come back . . . Mikayla was suddenly very afraid for Suzanne. Ramses was looking for any excuse to get back at the girls, and Suzanne stealing from him was all the reason he needed to throw her in a dungeon. How could someone so smart do something so stupid?

"We need your help," Mikayla said to Rigel. "Ramses is going to be impossible for us to deal with alone. He might not like you, but he hates us. You're our only friend in the summit."

"I wish I could," Rigel replied, "but Leo has called me back to Pyxis. I can leave those guards to protect you, but I have to attend to my king." Mikayla felt her stomach drop to her knees. That explained why Rigel was waiting at the entrance hall, dressed for travel.

"Why?" Brit demanded. "I thought you were here representing Pyxis."

Rigel made no efforts to hide the bitterness in his voice. "Leo isn't the ruler his sister was. His commands change with his moods. Apparently, he's thought the better of this conference and wishes me back at New Pyxia to help with the rebuilding. The messenger arrived this morning."

We should have stayed in Pyxis, Mikayla thought, but there was no time for that debate right now. They had to find Suzanne. If Rigel couldn't help them with that, then it was time to say good-bye. She asked him to fetch the guards from the tower. The way things were going today, they might need backup before the summit ended.

"Be safe," Rigel said to them. Mikayla thought it was a little late for that piece of advice.

It was near noon by the time they reached the summit, the sunlight red through the great stained-glass window. Mara waved to them. Mikayla felt guilt like a lump in her throat but ignored it. Finding Suzanne was all that mattered.

They were the last ones at the conference table and Ramses wasted no time pointing that out. "I'm glad the representatives from Zenith City could join us," he said. "But wait! One of you seems to be missing. Have you misplaced Suzanne?"

Mikayla bit back her words, taking her seat. Looking around the table, Suzanne wasn't the only one missing from yesterday. Besides Rigel, a scattering of the other representatives were gone as well. Mikayla was surprised to see that Burgrave's seat beside Ramses was also empty. Surprised, and a little dismayed; Burgrave was the most reasonable of Ramses's counselors.

"Well, now that we are mostly here," Ramses said, pausing to give Mikayla and Brit a gloating smile, "shall we begin?"

"Might I speak first?" Mikayla asked, doing her best to sound polite.

"Why certainly," Ramses replied.

Mikayla rose again and addressed the table. "Suzanne is missing," she said. "She disappeared last night." She turned toward Ramses. "If anyone knows where she is, you should tell us before we find out ourselves."

"Is that a threat?" Ramses asked. "You dare threaten me at my summit, in my own castle?"

Brit barked a laugh. "What are you gonna do, tough guy?" She grabbed the table by the edge. Before Mikayla could stop her, Brit flipped the whole table over. It was similar to how they had escaped from their trial in Zenith City, except the table in Fenhold was much larger. The NPCs seated across from them dove out of the way as the table slammed into the wall.

Well, shit, Mikayla thought. *So much for keeping things cool.*

"Are you mad?" Talleyrand shouted, his voice shaking.

"Shut up and sit down," Brit growled. Whimpering, the fat NPC picked up his knocked-over chair and sat back down.

Mikayla could hear footsteps outside in the hallway. They didn't have much time before Ramses's security showed up. She pulled her swords out of their sheaths and leveled one at the king.

"Tell me what you did with Suzanne," she said.

Ramses glanced over at Xenos before answering. Out of all the NPCs in the room, only Xenos had remained sitting when Brit flipped the table.

"Or what?" Ramses asked, his sneer slipping back into place. "Will you butcher me in my home, like you did to Lady Mara's people?"

Mikayla heard Mara gasp.

"What did you do to my people?" she asked.

"It wasn't us," Brit began to explain, but Ramses cut her off.

"They were invited into your keep as guests," he replied, his voice heavy with feigned dismay. "Once inside, they slaughtered your people and destroyed the keep. I am sorry, my lady. All of Altair grieves for them."

"That's not what happened at all!" Mikayla shouted. But she could see the fear in how the Altairi looked at her and Brit. "It was Gemini! Ramses's Assassin!"

"And what would I gain from murdering my own people?" Ramses asked.

"You think we just did it for kicks or something?" Brit asked incredulously.

"You helped devastate Altair during the war," the king said. "Unfortunately, Mara, when my forces arrived at your fort, there was nothing and no one left. Except for this."

Ramses withdrew one of Mara's flags from his inventory. It was tattered and singed, one of the blue rings burned through. Ramses set the flag on the table. It didn't prove anything. Brit knew that. But she saw Mara staring wide-eyed at the flag, her mouth drawn.

"My lady," Ramses drawled, "I am so very, very sorry."

Mikayla turned to Lady Mara, imploring the Paladin to believe her. "We tried to help them! But there were too many attackers and they set the inn on fire. You have to believe us. We were trying to help Joaquin defend them!"

"I will thank you not to speak his name," Lady Mara said, drawing her sword as she rose. "And I will thank you to accept my judgment for your crimes."

"It wasn't us!" But it was clear that Mara did not believe them. The door to the conference room burst open and a squad of Ramses's guard rushed in.

"Seize them!" the king shouted. The guards

advanced on one side and Lady Mara on the other.

"You take the guards," Mikayla told Brit. "I'll hold back Mara."

Brit nodded, grabbing up a chair and flinging it at the guards. It broke on a Defender's shield. Brit withdrew her halberd from her inventory, toppling the nearest guard with a single blow. Talleyrand led the charge of fleeing nobles. None of the guards seemed particularly eager to engage Brit, but Mikayla knew it was only a matter of time until more reinforcements showed up.

"Guard yourself!" she heard Mara cry. Mikayla turned just in time to deflect Mara's first slash. She thrust toward the Paladin but checked her blow; if she hurt Mara, it would only make them seem guiltier. She heard a cry of pain from behind her; she could only hope Brit was restraining herself as well.

If Mara saw Mikayla's mercy she paid it no mind. She stabbed directly at Mikayla's heart.

Mikayla caught Mara's blade between her two swords and turned it aside. But each time Mara stabbed forward, Mikayla took a step back, and soon she was backed up to the wall with nowhere else to retreat. And Mara had the size advantage, making it hard for Mikayla to simply dodge around her.

Mikayla slashed at Mara's head—slowly, so the Paladin had enough time to get out of the way. Lady Mara blocked with her gauntlet and lunged forward again. Mikayla jumped out of the way and Mara's sword grated against the stone wall.

Mikayla chanced a look at Brit and saw she was holding off the guards with wide swings of her halberd. Mikayla heard Mara yell, "Face me!" and turned back to catch the flat of Mara's blade in her face. The blow smacked Mikayla into the wall, banging her head against the stone. She stumbled to maintain her balance as her health bar dropped down.

Mara rushed her. Mikayla had nowhere she could retreat. Reflexes took over. Swinging over-hand, one of her swords drove Mara's into the floor. Her other blade came around, hitting Mara on the wrist in order to disarm the Paladin.

But her attack was too strong, her estoc too sharp. Mikayla felt her blade keep going, slicing through gauntlet and wrist, slicing up and slashing the now one-handed Paladin across the face.

Mara's sword clattered to the floor, her sword hand pixelating. She regarded her stump as she drew a hunting knife from her belt with her left hand. Mara threw herself forward, and instinctively Mikayla raised her swords to defend herself. Even if Mara saw, she was beyond caring. She spitted herself, Mikayla's blade stabbing through the Paladin's breast plate, directly in the center of the three blue rings.

"Oh," Mara whispered. Her features softened as she pixelated. She was at peace; then, she was gone. A tiny treasure chest appeared—Mikayla's reward for killing her.

"It wasn't us," Mikayla repeated. "We were trying to help them." But Mara was beyond hearing and Mikayla's words were lost in the stampede of more guards entering the room.

"I need a little help over here," Brit said. Mikayla snapped back to the moment and saw Brit was now surrounded. Sidestepping a fleeing noble, Mikayla stabbed one of the guards in the back, numb to the Altairi's cry of pain. Brit threw another guard out of the way, clearing the way between Mikayla and the window.

"We need to go," Mikayla said.

"Gotcha," Brit replied. She dropped her halberd and grabbed Mikayla. Before Mikayla could say "no," before she could even scream, Brit had thrown them backwards. The window shattered in a cloud of colored glass as they crashed through.

Brit's armor crunched against the ground. Mikayla slammed against her. Her whole body hurt. She pushed herself off Brit and got up. It was a relief when Brit found her feet a moment later. Already NPCs were shouting, and Mikayla could hear the guards rushing after them.

"Come on!" she shouted. She grabbed Brit's hand and pulled her toward the gate. They had to reach the portcullis before it closed. Arrows rained down from the battlements; the guards atop the wall were firing on them. Mikayla slashed them out of the air, dodging the ones she couldn't stop, but there were too many, and Brit was too big a target to miss.

The portcullis was down when they reached the gate. "Stand back," Brit said, readying a special move. Mikayla took her advice and got out of the way. Brit roared, throwing an Energite-fueled punch at the portcullis. Her fist ripped through the iron bars like they were paper. Grabbing the bars, Brit grunted and pulled, widening the gap so she could fit through. Mikayla slipped out after her, and then they were running into the Fenlands.

Mikayla could no longer hear the NPCs pursuing them. Still they ran. Vines whipped at their faces. The muck sucked at their feet. Mikayla felt none of that. All she could think was that they were running away from Fenhold, away from Suzanne, abandoning her to the cruelty of Ramses.